WITCH
ON THE BLOCK

MIDLIFE IN MOSSWOOD BOOK 1

louisa west romance

NEW WITCH ON THE BLOCK

MIDLIFE IN MOSSWOOD BOOK 1

LOUISA WEST

Edited by Kimberly Jaye

Proofread by Lindsay Aggiss

Cover design by Louisa West

For the Rosie in all of us.

If you don't like the road you're walking, start paving another one.

CHAPTER ONE

Rosemary listened to the sound of birds twittering outside of the bedroom window. She instinctively strained to hear the hum of traffic from a nearby expressway. A gentle breeze in the trees played harmony to the birdsong, and she could hear the faint sounds of someone chopping firewood not too far away. But that droning of cars and trucks that she had become accustomed to was gone.

She opened her eyes to an unfamiliar room. Her small suitcase stood, still packed, by the open bedroom door. Her daughter, Maggie, dozed on the bare mattress beside her, curled toward her mother for warmth and comfort. And as she reached out to stroke Maggie's soft dark curls, everything came rushing back to her.

The panicked snatch of what little personal belongings she would be able to carry. The hasty departure. Bundling a half-asleep Maggie into a cab. Urging the driver to *go* and slipping him cash she couldn't afford so that he would spirit them away into the night. Arriving in a strange town right on closing time for the local real estate office. Managing to secure a small, furnished cottage on the outskirts of town, no questions asked.

So many coincidences had to come together to make their escape from Randy a success—and Rosie was thankful for every one of them.

For all her adult life, she had been Randy's woman. In biker language, that meant she was his property. She moved when he said she could move, ate when he said she could eat. She did as she was told when she was told to do it, and above all, she kept her mouth shut.

At seventeen, running away with a man on a motor-cycle had been exciting. The freedom, the thrill of the road, the roar of the bikes between her legs. He'd promised to keep her safe, which was something she'd rarely felt in the foster homes she had passed through. It was just a damn shame she had been too naive to realize at the time that 'safe' also meant 'imprisoned.'

His promises and compliments soon gave way to yelling, broken things, and bruises. Then came the apologies, the promises to do better, and the reminders of how great their years on the road had been. The cycle left her so mentally exhausted that she didn't have time to think about leaving, much less act.

And then at twenty-nine, Maggie happened. She remembered sobbing over the toilet with Raquel and

Mimi when she read the pregnancy test. She could still hear Randy's voice when she told him.

"Guess you won't be runnin' out on me anytime soon, then, will ya?"

Letting out a tense sigh, Rosie unzipped her hoodie and shrugged it off. She laid it over Maggie, who snuggled into the soft material. First order of business: coffee.

The small tote bag of essentials she had brought sat on the white tile counter in the cabin's tiny kitchen. She didn't have the energy to inspect the place the night before. She waved dust from her face as she looked through the cabinets for something to make coffee with. She opened a cupboard to the left of the sink and found an old-fashioned kettle, wine glasses, *and* a dusty bottle of red wine. Jackpot!

She read the label on the bottle, cracked and peeling up at the corners.

FOX COTTAGE 1881
MUSCADINE

Well, alcohol was alcohol, cheesy labels or not. She turned on the kitchen tap and watched with a wrinkled nose as red-brown water spurted into the sink. *Gross,* she thought to herself. *How long had this place been vacant?* The water did eventually run clear, and she hoped the kettle would brew out any other impurities.

She set the kettle to boiling and decided to check out

the rest of the house. Starting at the front door, she meandered into the living room. It was a small but cozy rectangular room with a bay window overlooking the front yard and a little fireplace at the other end. The couches, rug, and curtains looked like they could use a good clean, and she could tell the mattress they had slept on needed an airing out. She started making a mental to-do list.

Fox Cottage had been vacant for some time, according to the realtor. It had been 'a while' since she'd done a showing of the property. The thick layer of dust on everything suggested her understatement was delib-erate—Rosie would be shocked if anyone had been in here in decades. But the owner would be so glad to have *any* rent coming in that the price was low, and improve-ments were welcome. It was fully furnished, which was useful for a family starting over, and the place was 'very private.' There was only one neighbor, a man who lived in a camper trailer an acre or so away.

Rosie took five steps from the living room to the breakfast nook, where a round table sat cramped in the corner. They might brush elbows, but Maggie could do her homework and the two of them could eat dinner, which was all they needed. The back hall was more like a hub and only hosted two doors. The one at the end of the hall revealed a small bedroom with a single bed and a strange round window that Rosie knew Maggie was going to adore.

The other door opened into a washroom. She gasped

with excitement to see a large claw-foot bathtub there, even though it was filthy. But her heart sank when she noticed the aluminum washtub and scrubbing board that substituted for a washing machine. Clearly, no one with children had lived here since the Civil War was a thing.

It would be a long while before Rosie would be able to afford a luxury like a washing machine. Right now, she wasn't even sure how she was going to pay her rent. She'd taken every cent from the meagre account Randy maintained with her for appearances and stolen the small roll of bills in his underwear drawer. But her funds acquisition had only netted her enough for a month's rent upfront and the bare essentials. And, Rosie knew it would spend quicker than it had come to her.

Her head churned with thoughts on how she was going to make this work. She would need a job, but who would hire her without a high school degree or any professional experience? With no credit, would the electric company even approve her as a new customer? Or a cell phone company give her a new contract, or a bank give her an account? Randy had controlled everything since she was seventeen. She didn't even know how to do most of these things, and she worried doing any of them might allow her husband to track her.

Her gaze eventually settled on the filthy bathtub. Well. She might as well get down to business. Living in a grungy cottage just would not do.

Rosie opened every single window in the house to harness the breeze in her efforts. She cleaned the old clawfoot tub with a ratty towel she found under the sink and some clumpy baking soda from the kitchen pantry. When she found a clothesline and bedsheets in the tiny linen closet in the washroom, she was so excited she didn't stop to think what might already be sleeping in them.

A palmetto bug. A palmetto bug was sleeping in them. The cockroach slash water bug, every bit as big as her thumb, was startled by her scavenging and flew—yes, *flew*—out of the linen closet in a panic. And like a yawn on a summer day, the panic was catching.

"Aaargh!!" Rosie made a sound somewhere between a scream and a strangled noise of indignation. She flung her hands to stop the roach from flying straight into her face and spun to swat at the sound of its huge wings flapping around her. It landed on the open windowsill, and it scrambled outside.

"Ugh!" She slammed the window behind it lest it get any more ideas, and then breathed heavily. Maggie joined her, bleary-eyed and with bed hair that would make a young Shirley Temple wild with envy.

"What are you *doing?*" she muttered, watching Rosie catching her breath. "It's like dumb o'clock."

It was about 9 am. Ten-year-olds could be so melo-dramatic. She knew she couldn't mention the giant cock-roach without Maggie sleeping in her bed for the next few days, so she skipped that story entirely.

"Getting a start on cleaning this place up!" she replied cheerily, hoping that some of it would rub off on

Maggie. It didn't. The child stood there, arms folded, looking for all the world as though she might turn tail and go back to bed.

"The sooner we have it all spic and span, the nicer it'll be to live here, right?"

Maggie quirked a brow. "Seems like it'll need a *lot* of spicking and spanning."

Rosie turned off the faucet on the tub and ushered Maggie out of the bathroom. "Good thing we're not afraid of hard work then, isn't it?"

Maggie slumped as she let herself be propelled through the house. "Can I at least have breakfast first?"

THE SUMMER SUN WARMED THEIR HEARTS AS WELL AS their skin as the pair set off for the small, sleepy-looking town that lay nestled in the valley below the cottage. Rosie squinted down the road that wound its way from Mosswood almost to her doorstep. It was a good thing that they both liked being outside; she only had to hear one instance of 'How much further?'.

Rosie took in the layout of the town. Residences clustered on the southwest side of town, with the commercial district hugged by a lazy river to the east. They passed by a large brick building that hulked over the intersection of the main road and the highway. A faded sign announced that Hayes Sugar and Syrup had once been a prominent fixture of Mosswood, but now the building looked abandoned.

"It's prolly haunted," Maggie announced. She peered at the building like a true Scooby-Doo connoisseur.

"Ya think?" Rosie asked, raising a brow.

"Duh. See the cobwebs in that broken window?" Maggie nodded her head in the direction of the building. "Dead giveaway."

Rosie hid a grin, resisting the urge to tease her child about how many spirits must be couch-surfing at Fox Cottage if cobwebs were a sign of ghostly presence.

The sweet smells of summer seemed more prevalent down here on the flats. Soft scents of magnolia blossoms mixed with the earthy aroma of long grass growing by the road. An old ranch-style house spruced up with white paint and green trim sat opposite the abandoned factory. A small, empty corral jutted out on one side of the building, with fields beyond it hosting two horses. A smart-looking sign nailed to the fence said it was the Mosswood Vet Clinic.

They continued down the highway, passing a squat little motel-slash-mechanical repairs shop call the Beep 'n' Sleep. It looked like a grease pit and had the smell to match. Granny's Diner on their right made Rosie's mouth water at the tempting scent of fresh fried chicken. A large but outdated sign out front said 'HAVE A GOOD SUMMER COYOTES' in big black removable letters. Old-school jukebox tunes drifted out of the drive-thru window. With a 'maybe' from Rosie that they could stop for milkshakes on the way back home, they stopped at the gates of Mosswood Elementary.

"So that's the new torture chamber," Maggie mused with a tone of long-suffering resignation. Rosie chuckled.

"I doubt it'll be all that bad, Pumpkin," she said.

Maggie wrinkled her nose, scuffing the toe of her sneaker across the blades of grass that poked up through the cracks in the old cement sidewalk. "Is this school gonna be full of rednecks?"

"That's not polite," Rosie schooled her. "Of course not."

"My last school had over six hundred kids. That school looks like it could barely fit twenty!"

Rosie rolled her eyes. Kids! "There are a hundred and thirteen students at Mosswood Elementary," she told Maggie with confidence. "I Googled it. Now c'mon, we got ourselves some explorin' to do!"

Main Street was a thin two-way road that was little more than a place for necessities to park themselves for consumption. A handful of people wandered along either side of the avenue in the shade from curbside trees. They took time out of their errand-running to rubberneck at the newcomers. Rosie put her arm around Maggie and ignored them.

The road seemed in good repair if a little weather-worn, with parking on either side. A single police cruiser sat outside a poky looking building that must have been the Sheriff's Department.

"Healthy critters!" a kid who looked like he lived in a swamp called out to them hopefully, gesturing at a battered bucket by his bare feet. He couldn't have been much younger than Maggie and didn't look half as well off as they were, which sure was saying something. "Itty bitty baby turtles! Ain't no pet like 'em," he said to Maggie as they continued down the sidewalk towards him. "Just fi' dollars'll get ya a turtle!"

Maggie immediately rounded on Rosie, eyes full, and hands clasped in front of her chest. "Can I get one, Mama?" she all but begged. "Look how cute they are!"

Rosie cringed. She couldn't think of anything worse than a slime-covered snake-with-a-shell stinking up their soon to be *de*-stinked cottage. She stepped forward reluctantly and peered into the bucket.

"I dunno that it's a good idea having them in a metal bucket on such a hot day," she told the kid, who seemed unperturbed by the welfare of his meal tickets.

"Naw," he shrugged before he sniffed and spat on the sidewalk. "They're reptiles – they like the warm. 'sides," he grinned, showing off that one of his front teeth were missing. "They'll sell like Granny's hotdogs on game day right sure enough. Fi'—"

"dollars. Yeah, I know," Rosie finished for him before turning to Maggie. "Sorry, Pumpkin, but we got ourselves some settlin' in do to first." She nodded at the kid and put her arm around Maggie's shoulder to guide her further down the street. "Maybe he'll have some for sale later on when we're ready to keep company."

Maggie didn't sulk for *too* long. Not ten steps further down the street, they found exactly what Rosie had been looking for.

A convenience store. *Hallelujah!*

They wandered into the aptly named Go-Go Mart through modern sliding doors. Like everywhere else in town, the place was immaculate, but it smacked of the city convenience stores that Rosie knew so well. It was a little slice of cosmopolitan living, right in the heart of the backwoods.

Maggie had already dashed for a display of teenage girl magazines she knew her mother would never buy. Rosie noticed an array of her favorite cosmetics that made her heart leap. Oh, thank goodness! She picked up two different face creams and held the tubes gratefully to her cheek, the way one would a puppy or a kitten, or a container of collagen filler after two days without one.

"Can I help you, ma'am?"

She froze and then looked over her shoulder. Yep, a man was talking to her, the crazy lady hugging face cream. She shoved them back onto the shelf and straightened her shirt as she turned to face him.

She glanced in Maggie's direction, hoping for back up. She could see two hands and the top of her daughter's humidified frizz around the cover of *Girlfriend*. Traitor.

"Oh," she said a touch too brightly in a last-ditch

attempt to cover her faux pas. "Well, um... yes. I suppose you could! You see, we're new in town, and—"

The man was younger than she was, had light brown hair, a handful of freckles across his nose, and kind green eyes. "You must be the folks that have rented Fox Cottage." He gave her the once over, and she suddenly wished she'd had something nicer to wear, or somewhere nicer to live. Carol-Ann hadn't mentioned that a reputation came hand in hand with her cheap rent.

Rosie hadn't wanted to announce their arrival in town, but she could see that the horse had already bolted. "We must be," she said, lifting a hand to brush her dark bangs out of her eyes.

"Rosie," she said then, because it was the least awkward and most logical thing to allow out of her mouth. She nodded in the direction of the magazine rack, her ponytail bobbing. "And that's my daughter, Maggie, short for Magnolia."

Ben glanced over. "Oh yeah?" he asked, feigning surprise. "Looks like Taylor Swift to me." Maggie peered over the top of the magazine before disappearing again. He held out a hand.

"I'm Ben Major," he smiled. He exuded an easy manner that she liked tremendously.

"Pleasure to meet you, Ben," Rosie said, resting her hands on her hips and taking a proper look around. She could see a display of vegetables in a market stall to the right, followed by fridges for meat. The rest of the store consisted of four narrow aisles that carried small household goods. She saw nothing that looked like fresh linen, much to her chagrin. The thought of sharing her bed with any other freeloading bugs was enough to turn her into an insomniac.

"I need some home staples. Food, of course," she smiled, "some decent coffee. I notice y'all don't seem to sell much in the way of homewares. Is there anywhere in town I can find stuff like that? And appliances," she added hastily. She was already dreaming of replacing the bathtub and scrubbing board with an actual washing machine of her very own.

Ben let out a low whistle. "Nothin' like that in Mosswood," he said apologetically. "'Cept for coffee makers." He stepped back to pat the top of a display of two 12-cup coffee brewers, which he seemed quite proud of. Rosie thought he had every right to be. Filtered coffee sounded divine after two days drinking it out of a kettle, grounds and all.

"Best advice I can give is to make a list and trek on out to Huntsville," he continued. "It's a ways north, but if you wait 'til you have a few things to get, it can make the trip worthwhile. They got Walmart, electrical stores, you name it. Only make sure you're back on the road home by four in the afternoon." He lifted his brows at her, indicating that this last pearl of wisdom was the most important of all. "Else you'll catch the *rush hour*."

Rosie felt her heart sink to the bottom of her chest. She wouldn't have minded being stuck in Huntsville's version of 'rush hour' if it meant that she could pick up a few things. But no car meant that she would need to rely on someone to give her a ride, and she intended to keep a low profile.

A cheap car that would make it possible to get around, or a washing machine? *Sigh.*

"I'll be sure and keep that in mind," she said, trying to hide her disappointment. "Thanks, Ben. Appreciate it."

"No problem," he said, seeming pleased to have been of service. "Now food and household *staples,* on the other hand—I can definitely help you out with those."

Maggie and Rosie left the Go-Go Mart almost twenty minutes later, each carrying two reusable shopping bags full of 'household staples.' They took a different route back to the highway to maximize their opportunity to explore. As they rounded the corner where Wallace Realty sat opposite the Town Hall, Rosie snuck a glance at the houses advertised in the windows.

There were some prettier places than Fox Cottage on Carol-Ann's listings, that was for sure. But Rosie had already started to feel an affinity for the rickety old pile that she couldn't explain. Beneath the dust and the ghost-heralding cobwebs, the place was a sanctuary by necessity. It was a haven for her and her daughter when they needed one most, and she had decided to do all that she could to repay it for giving them a fresh start.

Once they passed the realtor, they came across the Kwik Kleen. The laundromat that was little more than a bricked-in hallway with a door, but they pressed their noses to the windows like it was Disney World. Somewhere to do laundry that wouldn't leave her hands raw! And somewhere to lug laundry, on foot, every few days. She sighed.

Okay, she told herself. *The first thing I'm saving for is definitely a car.*

"Mom," Maggie said, interrupting her mental life-strategy planning session. "Look!"

Rosie turned her head in the direction Maggie was looking in. Tucked into a small back alley was a storefront painted with splotches of camouflage paint. Out front, there was some kind of rack that Rosie could only assume was for skinning dead animals, because there was a deer skeleton hanging from it limply, its bones bleached white by the sun. Her gaze jumped from the poor deer up to an imposing sign above the door.

OH SHOOT.

You got that damn right.

DINNER WAS A MAGNIFICENT AFFAIR OF JARRED-SAUCE spaghetti with a bowl of iceberg lettuce that served as a green salad. Maggie was flipping a pale green piece of leaf over and back before she caught her mother's eye across the table.

"Is Daddy coming to meet us here?" she asked. Though the question was commonplace, Rosie knew her daughter. She heard an undertone of fear in her daughter's voice and in the way she wouldn't meet her eyes. "Is this where we're living now?"

Rosie's food stuck in her throat. She'd kept them both busy on purpose that day. She expected Randy to start calling somewhere around mid-morning when he roused himself from his hangover in whoever's bed he'd fallen into. She had kept her cell phone turned off, so he wouldn't reach her. She continued to chew to buy herself some time before answering and then forced herself to swallow.

"This is where *we* are living now," Rosie said, measuring her words. "But he's not coming to live with us, Pumpkin. It's gonna be just you and me. Just us girls."

Maggie was quiet for a moment. "Is that because he's mean to us?"

Rosie's heart felt like it weighed a million pounds. "Yes," she said. "No more bad things are gonna happen from now on, okay?"

Maggie nodded, her dark hair bobbing up and down in her ponytail as she continued to eat her spaghetti. She had a halo of sauce around her lips, and Rosie wondered how on earth she could ask such wise questions and still manage to stain all her clothes with her dinner.

They cleared the plastic dishes they had bought at the Go-Go Mart, Maggie washing them clean while

Rosie dried and put them away. Between snippets of conversation, she looked out of the kitchen window towards the twinkling lights of Mosswood.

"I'll miss my old room and my friends."

"I know, Pumpkin," Rosie agreed. "But you'll be able to make some new friends, and it will start to feel like home before you know it."

"Except the air is nicer than home. It smells like Christmas here."

Rosie laughed, a rich, deep laugh that crinkled the corners of her eyes as she hugged Maggie to her. "That's because this is a pine forest!" she said, happiness bubbling inside her at the look of excitement on Maggie's face. "Maybe at Christmas time we can go and pick out our tree from a tree farm. Would you like that?"

"Heck yes!" Rosie's brow furrowed, and Maggie corrected herself. "I mean, yes, please – that sounds fun!"

Rosie's face fell into a 'that's-what-I-thought-you-said' expression. She took in a long breath and looked out of the window.

"Okay, then – we'll see." She let her eyes travel over the landscape in front of them while Maggie left for her bath.

It was strange, she thought, as she pulled the plug out of the kitchen sink. She'd spent less than 24 hours in this place, and she felt more at home now than she ever had in her whole life. Despite the house needing more attention than she'd bargained for, Rosie felt like she could make a life for them here. If she hadn't left the few friends she still had back home in Atlanta, the whole thing would have been perfect.

And then her phone lit up on the counter beside her. Before she could even question how it turned itself on, she saw Randy's name above a text message. With shaking hands, she picked up her cell.

'Guess u thought u could run out on me huh?'

Her breath was coming in short, ragged bursts. What if he knew where they were? What if he sent someone to come collect them—or, worse still, what if he came himself?

Rosie's heart thudded like a jackhammer. She didn't have time to register a second thought when her phone buzzed in her hand. She yelped and dropped it onto the counter. It fell face up, taunting her with a second message.

'U know u can't hide for long babe.'

Panic rose in her throat, cutting off her breath. She glared at her phone. All she wanted was to keep Maggie safe. She felt hot, her skin prickled, and nausea threatened to overtake her.

The phone vibrated on the counter again, but this time there was no text message. It shook, rattling against the worn tile surface. And then, right before her eyes, the phone screen split. Spiderweb cracks burst outwards in repeated pops that made the phone jump across the tiles. As it continued to skitter around like a cockroach trying to outlive a blast of bug spray, she noticed battery fluid bubbling out on the sides.

"Shoot!" she hissed, lunging for a pair of kitchen tongs that she'd just finished drying after dinner. She used them to pluck the phone from the counter and toss it into the trash can, leaving a trail of iridescent ooze dripping behind it.

What the actual fuck?

Rosie swiped at the ooze with a kitchen cloth and then threw that in the trash too. She felt exhausted, her long dark hair falling over her shoulder as she leaned on the counter to steady herself. She breathed in through her nose and then let the air out through her mouth, feeling her presence of mind starting to creep back to her.

The sound of Maggie pulling out the bath plug dragged her back into the moment.

"Mom!" Maggie called from the bathroom. "Can you please comb through my hair?"

"Sure, Pumpkin," Rosie answered a touch too quickly. She took another deep breath, and then another, letting the action flow through her, slow her heart rate, and calm her mind.

She knew that there were posts all over the internet about phones exploding, but there was no way to explain what she had just seen *her* phone do.

CHAPTER TWO

The next day, Rosie and Maggie carried two full bags of laundry into town to the Kwik Kleen. Maggie sat on a bench across the street under a large tree and read her book. Rosie could see her clear enough from the laundromat and worked hard to calm her nervous maternal instinct. Maggie needed to develop and flex her independence, and she knew it, but she could do it where Rosie could keep an eye on her.

With a bag in each arm, she stepped inside Clean Clothes Heaven. The place was empty, and she sighed with relief as she burst through the glass door. It was colder inside, owing to the window AC units that blew thin strands of ancient plastic in a weak salute to summers in Georgia.

There was a small outdoor-style bench seat directly beside the AC, and then two washing machines and dryers side-by-side on each wall. They seemed to be facing off against each other from across the divide of cheap linoleum.

Rosie dumped one bag of laundry into the machine on her right and clicked the door closed. She turned to repeat the process on the left when the first door popped back open again. She grunted, reaching to close it with an ankle while stuffing her underwear into the other one. She wasn't quite coordinated enough and gave up, shoving her smalls into machine number two. She turned to check there weren't too many clothes for the first one to stay closed. It would be just her luck to have brought three loads of washing to town instead of two.

But there didn't seem to be a space problem. Rosie leaned closer to the inside of the machine, gave her clothes an experimental prod, and then closed the door. The second machine popped open behind her, slapping lighting against her derriere.

"Argh!" she yelped, almost jumping out of her skin before she turned to glare at the handsy washing machine. She frowned, placing a comforting hand on her butt out of habit. Of *course* the machines would be so old that they were practically defunct. Tutting with irritation, Rosie shoved her underwear into the second machine for the second time. She heard what she thought to be the beginnings of a now-familiar *pop* behind her, and her hand shot out to slap the door of the first machine closed before it could barf out her clothes again.

After a full two seconds of crouching with her arms outstretched, struggling to hold both doors closed at once, Rosie sighed. She couldn't put in her laundry soap, and she could not reach the change in her pocket, either. Resisting the strong urge to cuss, she let go of both doors and stood.

She dug into her pocket and braced herself for the pool of laundry about to flood at her feet. But both doors remained closed. With raised brows, Rosie held her change in one hand and the remains of her dignity in the other. She popped the changed into machine one, waiting for it to give her some sign that it was powering up.

It didn't. It ate her change, and all but burped in her face.

Rosie did like to think of herself as a good person. She wasn't overly devout, but she only swore when the occasion called for it. This occasion was starting to call for the more morally dubious parts of her vocabulary. Deciding to cut her loss and use one of the other two machines, she bent to retrieve her clothes.

The door of the machine refused to budge. She took a long, steadying breath, and then jerked on the door with abandon.

"Give. Me. Back. My. Clothes!!"

She managed to get it open, but not without sacrificing the skin on the knuckles of her right hand to the laundry gods. When two machines were finally humming along, she collapsed onto the nearby bench.

She picked up a copy of a nearby magazine to fan her sweaty self with. When at last her heartbeat had returned to normal, and the window ACs had cooled her sweat, she turned her attention to the magazine. The Herald of Hope was little more than a newsletter printed into a booklet by the local church. A power couple stood smiling on the front cover.

Rosie supposed he was good-looking if you liked thin, intellectual types. His wife looked manic in a wide-eyed 'imitation of Jackie Onassis' way. The pair of them wore matching aprons that said 'Cooking for Jesus', and a crowd of people flanked them, wielding huge smiles and kitchen utensils.

Rosie huffed through her nose.

She got up to have a look at an over-burdened community noticeboard on the wall. It was full of advertisements of puppies for sale, or for the Beep 'n' Sleep, or notices from the county. Then a piece of yellow paper with the words **HELP WANTED** in bold black marker caught her eye.

Seeking p/t employee for Mosswood Go-Go Mart.
Must be able to work various hours as required.
Previous experience not necessary.

The handwriting was messy and hurried, and the ink of the phone number scrawled along the bottom of the page still looked wet. Raising a brow at the prospect, Rosie tore the ad from the pin and stuffed it in the back pocket of her jeans. On second thought, she also tore a tab from a purple flyer advertising babysitting services.

Getting a job would take so much pressure off. She was already worried about what was going to happen if she couldn't make next month's rent. The cottage was coming along—at the very least, she hadn't run into anything else living there—but it would be good to buy a few things for the place if she could ever get a ride to Huntsville.

Then, once they settled and she was working, Maggie could do some chores to earn herself some pocket money. Rosie would never allow Maggie to be at the mercy of anyone else's charity like she had been. Particularly not anyone that didn't have much by mercy or charity themselves.

LATER THAT DAY, ROSIE ADMIRED THE CLEAN DRAPES she had re-hung when she heard a knock on her front door. Worry creased her brow, and her heart rate skipped up a gear. She could only think of one person who would come knocking on her door, and he most certainly wasn't welcome.

"D'you think she's home?" The voice was hesitant but feminine enough to allay some of Rosie's initial panic. But Randy could be quite resourceful, and she wouldn't put it past him to send others to do his bidding. She knew how his twisted mind worked.

"How should I know?" another person replied.

A third voice chimed in, "I hope she's nice."

Through the drapes around the front window, Rosie saw three well-dressed ladies standing huddled together on her porch. She considered pretending not to be home. The fewer people in town who knew she and Maggie were even living here, the better. She stepped back and listened.

"Carol-Ann Wallace told me this morning that she's *trim*."

"She lives *here*?" Rosie recognized the middle woman by her pert nose and coiffed hair from the front page of the Church magazine. "On the outskirts of town, surrounded by creepy woods? Sounds like she could use a little Jesus if you ask me."

Rosie made up her mind to tiptoe back to the kitchen. But then, the church lady stepped over to the window and cupped her hands to look between the drapes—and right at Rosie.

"Well, hi there!" the woman chirped in a loud voice that she seemed to hope would drown out her previous bitchiness. Rosie groaned to herself. Why hadn't she stayed in the damn kitchen like a *normal* person in hiding?

Resigning herself, Rosie went to answer the door. At the last second, she leaned to grab her keys so she could pretend to be on her way out if needed.

"Hi," she offered the three women as she stepped onto the porch. Their eyes swept over her, taking in her messy ponytail, cutoff jeans, and a band t-shirt she'd had since high school. She felt as though she was being judged from every angle – because she *was* – so Rosie mustered a forced smile.

"So glad we caught you!" the nosy window-looker sighed, sounding excited. "I'm Priscilla Bishop, but everybody calls me Prissy." She pressed a hand sporting a huge sparkling wedding set to her chest. "This is Leanne Coombes," she indicated a thin woman in a powder blue sweater on her right, "and this is Tammy Holt." A shy-looking plump lady offered an awkward wave.

Prissy looked like an ad for a whitening toothpaste commercial, the way she wouldn't stop smiling. "Consider us your *official* Mosswood welcome wagon!"

She said it with such gusto that Rosie half expected there to be a trumpet fanfare in the seconds that followed. She lifted her arms to either side of her and let them plop back down, which was as much enthusiasm as she could muster.

"Consider me officially welcomed." The women tittered polite laughter. "I'm *trim*, apparently," she said as she offered her hand for a shake. "Though these days I mostly just go by 'Rosie.'"

Prissy looked shocked for half a moment but recovered gracefully. "Oh, gosh! Color us embarrassed!" She shook her head at herself. "I guess that's why the good book warns us against gossipin', isn't it?"

"Well, I won't start throwing stones if you don't,"

Rosie offered with a small smile. She could not afford to make enemies here, even if her neighbors *were* nosy busybodies. But a little reminder of all the *other* things the good book warned against wouldn't go amiss.

Prissy laughed. "In a house this tiny, I don't guess you can afford to!"

"Yes," Leanne said, gesturing at the grubby surroundings with a look of false pity on her thin face. "How are you finding the place? Looks like it needs a *lot* of work!"

"I admire your fortitude," Prissy cut her friend off, shaking her head in mock admiration. "You're clearly not afraid of a little elbow grease!"

All three women were now stealing glances at the house beyond her, trying to gather clues about her life.

"I'm sure it will keep me busy," Rosie said, stepping out onto the porch and closing the door behind her. Prissy recovered first.

"Oh, busy's the only way to be!" she chirped.

"Prissy's only the busiest woman in Mosswood," Tammy chimed in. "She's the head of the PTA, president of our sewing circle – *and*," Tammy drawled, making it clear that she'd left the best for last, "She's married to Pastor Bishop." Tammy sighed in a way that said she wouldn't mind being married to the pastor herself.

"We're all members of the congregation at Hand of God Southern Baptist," Leanne added.

Rosie lifted her chin as she realized where this was

going and jingled her keys by way of excuse. "It's so kind of y'all to stop by like this, but I'm just on my way out."

"Oh, we totally understand!" Prissy crowed, so thrilled to play a round of Southern Hospitality that she didn't miss a beat. "We'll only take up a moment of your time. We're just here to invite you to join us this Sunday," she lowered her voice. "It would be such a nice way for you to meet everyone and introduce your little one to the other kids in town. You have a daughter if I'm not mistaken?"

She barely felt like she had time to get a word in edgewise. "Yes, Maggie."

"Well, she is just gonna love Miss Hattie, our Sunday School teacher. All the kids do. And it's such a relief knowing they're making the right kinds of friends when they're in church, isn't it?" Prissy nodded her head sympathetically.

"Um, well—"

"Tammy, here, is the head of the choir if you're interested, and LeeAnn runs our newsletter. We brought you a copy." She handed over the newest edition of the Herald of Hope. Prissy and the same man were on the cover, this time washing cars.

"Look, that's really nice—" Rosemary said, but Prissy interrupted.

"Nonsense! What kind of people would we be if we didn't invite our new neighbor to join in fellowship with us?" She shook her head with that fake smile still on full

29

blast. "Sunday service starts at nine, and we sure hope to see you there. And if you can't make it, not to worry. It's on the local radio station every Sunday."

The local radio station, Rosie thought? *Lord help me.*

Prissy stepped off the porch, and the other two women followed without her having to say anything else. "Now, we're just gonna get out of your hair and let you get back to your runnin' around!"

"Thanks for stopping by," Rosie called. She was more drained by those few minutes than she had been by a full day of cleaning!

Tammy didn't get very far down the yard before she turned as though she had just remembered something. "I meant to ask," she began, "Ms. Wallace—over at Wallace Realty—mentioned that there's no man around the house?"

Rosie couldn't stop her signature sarcastic eyebrow from quirking. "That's right," she said. "And no plans to have one join us anytime soon."

"Oh," Tammy corrected herself with a shy smile, "I didn't mean that. I just meant, well, would it be alright if I sent my husband down to offer a hand with things around here? He's real handy."

Rosie stood up straighter at the first real friendliness any of the three women had shown her. "I'm sure I could find something for him to do." She tilted her head as she inspected the other woman and returned her smile. "Thanks."

Tammy smiled wider, as Prissy took a step back toward them. "Why, Tammy, you really are the sweetest thing! And she's the best babysitter in Mosswood, even though she doesn't have any of her own." Prissy placed a hand on Tammy's forearm. "But never mind, dear. The good Lord blesses us all in different ways, I'm sure."

Tammy looked as though she'd been punched in the gut, and in a way, Rosie supposed she had. Prissy's punishment for unsanctioned Christian-ing was certainly swift. She felt a profound sadness roll off the plump woman as she turned to follow Prissy to a large white SUV. The horn beeped as Prissy unlocked it and began to climb into the cab.

"You let us know if you need anything!" she called before slamming the driver's side door.

As she watched the expensive ride take off down her driveway, there were two things Rosie knew for sure. Prissy Bishop was the most influential woman in town. And, Rosie thought as she unlocked the door and went back inside, she didn't like her one bit.

FRESH NIGHT AIR SOOTHED HER FRAYED HEART AS ROSIE swayed on the porch swing that hung in front of Fox Cottage. The chains creaked as she pushed off with her toes, one leg curled beneath her, a glass of wine cradled in her lap. The cicadas in the trees would ramp up their song like an old car struggling to start, and then once one got going, the rest would join in, humming all together in a high-pitched buzz until they sputtered out one by one and waited for the conductor to wind them up again.

The wine was the one she had found in the cabinet, with the funky label meant to look antique. She had expected the wine to taste like straight vinegar, but it must have been well-preserved in the back of the cabinet despite the warm weather. It even felt cold in the bottle. She felt her nervous energy dulling and hoped tonight, finally, she might be able to get some decent sleep.

She was peering out into the inky blackness of the forest surrounding the cottage when she froze. The warm cozy feeling from the wine and the cicada song melted away.

A man was standing in the shadows by the magnolia tree at the end of her drive.

If it were any later in the evening or she'd had more than three sips of wine, she might have thought she imagined it. But the shadow's shoulders were too broad to be part of her imagination. As she reached to switch off the porch light to improve her night vision, the guy stepped out of the darkness. He made his way up the drive towards the house.

Ice flooded Rosie's veins. The man was tall—*really* tall. Much too tall to be Randy, but he could be someone Randy sent.

Her grip on her glass slipped. It fell to the deck and

smashed, and Rosie, who was barefoot, stepped back away from the glass. She looked back up at the approaching shadow.

If this dude, whoever he was, wanted trouble, then she would rather find out sooner than later. She summoned every ounce of strength she possessed and lifted her chin in defiance.

"Can I help you?" she called across the darkness between them, hearing his boots crunch on the gravel as he approached. A light chuckle drifted towards her from his direction.

"I'm the one who's supposed to be helpin' *you,* darlin'." His words slurred together, and he had such a strong Irish accent that she took a second to make out the words. "But thanks very much for the offer."

"Well then," she said, "that's easy! You can help me by getting the *fuck* off my property."

He stepped into view, revealed by the golden porch light spilling over him. He *was* tall – more than six feet, she guessed. His broad shoulders hunched as he walked, his thick arms ending in hands stuffed into his pockets. His trunk was sturdy rather than trim like a starving Hollywood actor, as though he had come by his bulk through honest labor rather than striving for fashion. He swayed as he shuffled closer to the porch.

"Such language from a lady," he tutted. "You'll have to be calming down the cursing when ya crowned."

She'd been fixing to let loose a string of cuss words

that would make a sailor blush when he threw her for a loop.

"Crowned?" she asked, arching an eyebrow high. Clearly, he was drinking much stronger stuff than she was.

"Aye." He rested one boot on the bottom step of her porch, the smell of whiskey wafting up to greet her. He dipped his head, extending one hand in a theatrical gesture. "Not long now, my Queen."

He threw his head back, his voice ringing out like a bell in the cool night air. "We'll unite our kingdoms and fulfill the prophecy at last!"

Rosie glared at him for a long moment. Who *was* this guy? And then she remembered what Carol-Ann had said about the neighbor in the camper trailer. She stood up straighter. *Oh.* She would have to remember to get onto Carol-Ann for her little white lies. She had been expecting a beer-bellied old hunter type, not Beefcake O'Whiskeybreath over here.

"Prophecy. Right..." She went to take a step backward towards the door, and then remembered the broken glass on the deck. She glanced down to find a clear path, and when she looked up, he had leaped up the porch steps and was standing beside her.

"Allow me, my love," he murmured before scooping her up in his thick, muscled arms. He swayed with the effort, and she thought he was going to topple over with her in tow.

"What—the—*fuck?*" Rosie barked, punctuating

each word with a slap to his head. He leaned backward to prevent further attack, and she was sure they were going overboard. "Put me *down!*" she commanded, straining to get free of him.

"Steady now! I can't have ya cuttin' your pretty little feet," he insisted.

"And *I* won't be molested on my own damn porch!" In desperation, Rosie snatched at the handle of the broom she'd left out earlier that day. She jabbed the end of it into his chest, making him grunt. She stumbled out of his grip and onto the deck, barely avoiding the broken glass.

"Molestin'," he breathed, rubbing the sore spot on his meaty chest. "Nobody said anythin' about *molestin'.*" He held up his hands. "I'll behave, scout's honor. That is," he grinned, "unless you decide you be *wantin'* me to misbehave."

His big hands skimmed the collar of his dark green button-down shirt, and he began to undo the top buttons. His roguish grin tugged the corner of his mouth further on one side and revealed deep laugh lines around his eyes.

For the first time, she got a good look at his face. His hair was a dark, rusty red, and he had a trimmed beard to match. His nose was too big and crooked, as though it had healed on its own more than once. Rosie felt that he looked familiar somehow, but she couldn't place him.

So, she hit him square in the face with the bristles of her broom instead.

"Ow!" he howled. Her ninja-broom skills had the desired effect—he backed up and clutched at his nose. Rosie skittered to the doormat and pressed her backside to the door, keeping him at bay by wielding her weapon.

"Shh!" she hissed again, "I have a sleeping kid inside, and if you wake her, it'll be the last thing you ever do."

He was rubbing the bridge of his nose, looking at her with a hurt expression. "I think ya broke my nose!"

"It was crooked enough to begin with," she fired back. "I doubt anyone'll notice."

"Hey!"

Rosie shrugged a shoulder and tightened her grip on the broomstick so that she could wave it menacingly.

The man held up both hands and took a begrudging step backward. "Lemme ess-plain," he said, his words running together. "You're me crafty mistress."

Rosie blinked. Having conversations with drunk Irishmen had never been on her list of things to do for fun. "Say what now?"

"A mistress of the craft!" he corrected himself, holding up a finger to show that he remembered.

"The *only* thing that I'm the mistress of," Rosie warned, "is kicking your sorry ass. Now shoo!" She swatted him with the broom again. He stepped back to avoid the swipe and grinned when he was successful. But then he lost his balance, tumbling backward down the porch steps. He reached for the railing to save himself and only just managed to stay on his feet.

"Oh, darlin'," he breathed with a wolfish grin, "I *like* me a woman with a bitta fire to 'er."

"Oh, barf," she shot back.

Rosie narrowed her eyes as he turned and began the walk across the lawn in the direction he had come from. She intended to watch him until he was no longer in sight—just to make sure that he actually left—but he seemed to melt into the shadows. Unnerved, she fumbled behind her back for the door handle and let herself back into the house, locking the door and dead-lock once she was safe.

That was her neighbor? *Great.*

CHAPTER THREE

Another day, another pilgrimage into town. Now that everything felt more familiar, Rosie was able to pay attention to details about the town that she'd missed. There was a cute as heck little hardware store, Wood & Wax, behind and to the right of Granny's. With the state of the cottage, she could tell she was likely to become one of their best customers. She wondered if they had any kind of rewards program so that she could save a few bucks here and there.

She noticed the unmistakable scent of fresh doughnuts on the light breeze that wafted up Main Street from the river. It seemed to be coming straight from the Sheriff's Department. Maggie, a veritable bloodhound for anything even remotely resembling junk food, sniffed the air experimentally as they stepped into the Go-Go Mart.

"Wanna go choose the cereal you'd like, Pumpkin?"

Rosie asked before Maggie could get distracted by the magazine rack again. "I'll be along in a minute."

"Okay!" Maggie darted for the cereal aisle as Ben stepped out of a door to the left of the counter. The movement caught Rosie's eye. She glanced past him to see the closet-like room with a desk housing an ancient computer, shelves, and mountains of paperwork.

"Well, howdy Miss Rosie," he said with a smile, slipping his thumbs into his belt loops as he approached her. "What can I do ya for?"

"Hi Ben," Rosie said, returning his smile. She reached into the pocket of her jeans, fiddling with the piece of paper she had torn off the Kwik Kleen notice-board. She didn't know why she'd brought it with her. It wasn't like he was going to want proof of his advertisement. "I—uh. I found a want ad at the laundromat, and I wondered if you were still looking for someone?"

He raised his eyebrows. "Sure, we're still looking. Do you have any experience?"

Rosie felt her heart sink. For over 22 years, she'd been little more than Randy's cook and housemaid. "The ad said no experience necessary," she mumbled.

"That's right," Ben said. "I'm just curious is all."

She needed this job. At the rate the stupid washing machines at the Kwik Kleen were chewing through her change, soon she'd be out of luck.

But more than needing the money, Rosie felt like she wanted to work there. It would feel good to be gainfully employed, earning her own money, and building a life without relying on Randy's whims to see her through. She took a breath.

"Look." She took a breath and then plunged into the unknown. "I'ma be real with you," she said to the guy. "I need this job. I'm new in town, and I got a daughter to raise and rent to pay. What that means is that I will work hard for you. I will be on time, and I will be reliable. I won't ditch shifts, and I'm willing to work any extra shifts you feel like slingin' my way." She smiled again, but this time it was matter-of-fact.

The guy looked at her as though weighing his options. Finally, he nodded. "Fair enough. You're hired."

A deadweight lifted from her shoulders. "Really?!" She grinned – her first, fully-fledged Mosswood smile. "When can I start?"

To Rosie, the dusty highway shoulder she and Maggie walked down might as well have been clouds. She couldn't believe her luck – managing to get a job on her fifth day in town was almost too good to be true. But she wasn't about to look a gift horse in the mouth. Instead, she chose to take it as a sign that things were finally starting to turn around for her and Maggie.

Maggie babbled happily about the heat, the smell of grass, and anything else her butterfly-like brain settled on. The rumble of a truck coming up behind them prompted her to guide them further onto the shoulder, lest Maggie fail to notice at all.

But the vehicle didn't pass them and chug on out of town. Rosie heard the gears shifting down and turned to look over her shoulder as a battered red pickup crawled beside them. A thick forearm with a sleeve rolled up to the elbow was parked in the open window. As the truck drew level with them, she could see that it was her new neighbor behind the wheel.

Here we go, she thought.

"Fancy meetin' you here," he smiled down at the pair of them. Rosie sighed. The last thing she needed was to have to try and explain to Maggie how she knew the wild-haired Irishman.

"Hi!" her gregarious youngster piped up. Rosie side-eyed her, and Maggie moved closer to her mom, peering up at the truck.

"Hello," Rosie finally conceded, taking a breath as though to ready herself for a repeat of his antics on her porch the other night.

He tapped his fingers on the peeling paint of the door, a knotted leather bracelet jiggling around his wrist. "Headin' home?"

Rosie shrugged a shoulder, her eyebrow rising. Where the heck else would they be going? "Yep," she said, feeling more awkward by the minute.

"We're headed the same way, and the day's not gonna get any cooler. I can give you a lift if ya like."

She hesitated, torn between the allure of escaping

the heat of the asphalt and having to put up with more of this guy's antics. Her mind was made up for her by Maggie, who uttered a soft "Please, Mom?" behind her. "The milk's getting warm."

Dagnabbit.

"That's very neighborly of you," Rosie said. Accepting would give her the perfect opportunity to chat with him about the other night. If that meant they got the milk home sooner, then all the better. "Thanks."

"Not a bother," he replied with a smile. He leaned across the bench seat in the truck to open the passenger side door for them from the inside.

Rosie walked Maggie around the front of the truck and bent to help her daughter up before thinking better of it. She climbed up herself so that she was sitting next to the stranger and then reached down to give Maggie a hand.

"Don't forget ya seatbelts," he said.

The inside of the truck smelled like leather soap and fresh coffee, which gave Rosie a hankering for a cup herself. It roared up the highway, made the turn at the sugar mill, and began the steady climb into the woods. Fields gave way to lean juvenile pines, then a mature pine forest with sparse undergrowth. The road wound through the woods until the drive opened out into the small clearing where Fox Cottage sat.

They pulled up on the lawn by the house. Rosie jumped down after Maggie and handed her the grocery bag. "Could you go put these away, Pumpkin? I'll be along in a minute."

Maggie clearly wanted to stay and listen in on the grown-up conversation but nodded. "Okay."

"Thanks, hon," Rosie said. Maggie dashed into the house like a bat out of hell, to minimize her chances of missing the whole conversation. Rosie turned to her neighbor, who had climbed out of the truck.

"Look," she said, holding out one hand to stop him when he opened his mouth. "Since we're neighbors, I'm gonna give you some friendly advice."

His eyebrows had lifted as though pulled by invisible strings, but Rosie didn't care. She needed to say this, and he needed to hear it.

"Don't be coming around my place drunk like that. I've got a kid. If you do it again, I'll call the cops." She warmed to her subject. "In fact, don't be coming around at all unless you're invited. And none of that 'King and Queen' stuff in front of her – she's been through enough without having to listen to that."

She finished laying down the law, her hands having crept to her hips as she'd talked. Now that she finished, she flicked her long dark ponytail back over her shoulder.

He took her in for a few seconds, his eyes almost the same kind of green as sea glass. He pursed his lips and nodded once.

"Fair enough," he said at last, before holding out his hand. "Declan Forrest."

It was her turn to lift a brow, but she reached for his hand anyway. It completely enveloped hers and was warm. Not as rough as she'd expected it to be. She felt some kind of tingling sensation in her palm as it connected with his, and it was almost enough to make her frown. It wasn't romantic – it was more like a buzz of energy.

"Rosie Bell," she replied, her shake firm for two pumps before she took her hand back. She slipped her hands straight into the pockets of her jeans to rid herself of the strange sensation.

"At ya service, Rosie," Declan replied, offering a brief but friendly smile before turning back to his truck. "I'm right on through the woods that way." He jutted his chin to the north-east. "If ya need anythin', just holler."

"Thanks," she said. "I'll do that. And thanks again for the lift. We appreciate it."

"No worries." He stepped up into the truck and rumbled off down the drive.

AFTERNOON SUN FLOODED THE OVERGROWN FRONT YARD of Fox Cottage. After a full day of work at the Go-Go Mart and walking the distance to town and back, Rosie was tired. Maggie chatted as they sat together, drinking home-made milkshakes on the porch, both barefoot and smiling.

"I wonder if there's an ice cream shop in town."

Maggie sipped her milkshake. "Or a pizza place! Did you see that huge park the other day, Mom?"

"Kinda," Rosie said, leaning on the railing and running her eyes over the weed-filled garden beds. "Maybe we can check it out tomorrow when I finish my shift."

"And see if there's an ice cream shop?" Maggie asked, her hazel eyes brightening at the thought.

"Maybe," Rosie replied. "You can tell me which flavor you might choose while we pull some weeds."

Maggie groaned. "Do I have to?"

Rosie almost smiled at the familiar tone of a preteen whine but stopped herself just in time. She'd already padded down the steps onto the dirt path leading to the cottage, and the warm raw earth beneath her feet felt like heaven. She squinted up at her daughter.

"You don't ever have to do anything you don't wanna," she said, raising her milkshake cup to her lips. She peered at Maggie over the rim. "But I hope that you'll pitch in with this. This place is our new home, and I'd like to stay here for a long while. Wouldn't you?"

"Sure," Maggie said, glancing up at the moss trailing from an ancient oak tree in the middle of the lawn. "It's nice."

Rosie smiled, finished her milkshake, and moved to set her cup on the top step of the porch for now.

"If you think it's nice now, imagine it weed-free. Think of all the beautiful flowers we would have room to plant in these beds. And we could make a cute stone path, leading to the porch." She held out a hand to Maggie, who grinned and took it.

A half-hour later, they had finished one garden bed but still had four more to do. The sun was beginning to dip below the high canopy of the surrounding woods, and Rosie's mind had turned to what to fix for dinner. Maggie stretched.

"Can I have a bath now?" She lifted her dirty hands and wriggled her fingers at Rosie, who laughed.

"Sure. You know how to set it up."

The sound of the washroom taps lulled her as she piled the garden waste into a corner of the yard. She'd check the rules on burning off some leaves tomorrow. Later on, they could have a small bonfire and make s'mores—one of Maggie's favorite things.

A low rumble sounded from down the track leading up to the house, and Rosie's head snapped towards the noise. Before long, a silver pickup truck pulled into the clearing. A man parked it on the edge of the drive, smiling as he started up the lawn towards Rosie.

"Well, hi there," he called, wiping his hands on his jeans as he approached, and then offering one to Rosie once he was closer. She hesitated and then held her hands up so he could see that they were dirty. He nodded in acknowledgment.

"You must be Miss Bell. I'm Terry Holt. I own the hunting shop in town, Oh Shoot. You've met my wife, Tammy."

Rosie lifted her chin in recognition. So, this was shy Tammy's husband, and thanks to Prissy Bishop, Rosie knew that they'd had trouble having kids.

"I did," Rosie said with a nod. Though she didn't know either of them well, she was a little surprised to imagine shy but fashionable Tammy with someone so gregarious. "She was good enough to call on me the other day."

Terry smiled. "That's my Tammy. Sweet as molasses." He gestured at the yard. "She mentioned that you might need a little help with some things around the place. I've just come from Huntsville. Thought I'd stop in on my way back home and see if I could be of any assistance."

His smile, which until then had been polite and genial, took on a devious cast. Rosie thought she noticed his eyes skim down from her face to her décolletage, but when she blinked, he looked as friendly as he had two minutes before.

"Actually," she said, not stubborn enough to turn him down, "I have a garden bench that I can't lift on my own. Would it be too much—"

"Not at all," he cut her off, putting his hands on his hips in a that-suits-me-down-to-the-ground gesture. "Beautiful woman like you, without a man around the house to fix what needs attention. Hell," he grinned, "it'd be my pleasure."

When Rosie didn't immediately respond to his idle

flirtation, he continued. "Just point me in the right direction."

He held out his hand, indicating for her to walk ahead. Again, Rosie hesitated. She felt uncomfortable walking in front of him, so she forced a smile and began to walk so slowly he had no choice but to walk beside her.

On a slope that was the beginnings of what the locals called The Ridge, a rusted garden bench rested upturned. Ivy had conquered the twisted iron, reclaimed by the spirit of nature that seemed to surround the cottage itself.

"I'd like it up by the house. Do you think it's too heavy for the both of us?"

Her question was genuine, but for some reason, it made Terry smirk. An uneasy feeling churned in Rosie's stomach.

"I think we oughta be just about able to handle it," he said, ripping the ivy from the bench before waving his hand at Rosie. "You take that end. I'll walk backwards—don't let me fall, now," he chuckled.

Rosie quirked a brow and lifted. The bench was very heavy, and she strained with the weight as Terry adjusted his grip. "Let me know if you need to rest," he said, and they were moving before Rosie knew it.

After all his talk of 'no man around' and his little smirk, Rosie had no intention of asking for a break, even if she did need one. She clenched her teeth as they walked the bench over to the old oak tree in the middle of the lawn, facing the drive. They put it down, and he let out a deep breath.

"Hoo boy," he laughed, oblivious to the thunder in Rosie's look. "She's not a pretty girl, but she's solid as hell."

Rosie crossed her arms. "She'll be pretty enough, once I put my stamp on her."

Terry's gaze narrowed, and the corners of his lips turned up in a lazy smile. "Now that I don't doubt for a minute, Miss Rosie."

She felt again that same discomfort she kept questioning. Was he just being a hospitable Southern gentleman? Or was he a Southern rogue pushing her boundaries, to find out how far she was willing to push boundaries herself?

"Been a while since I've been on this property," he said, fingers riding in his belt loops as he turned to look around them. "Used to be a little trellis over here with an old grapevine, though I don't expect it's still growing anything anymore. Been quite a while since anyone's taken care of it."

He began walking up a small incline, and she reluctantly followed. As they walked, he explained all the local landmarks – particularly those around Fox Cottage. It was clear that he was a woodsman, as though owning a hunting and fishing supply store hadn't tipped her off to that already.

"Used to be, you could see the river through here. Wonder if you still can." He stood at the highest point on the property and looked in the direction of the river-bank. "There!"

Uninvited, he took a step nearer to her and leaned over her, pointing in the direction of the river. She could feel his knee behind hers and knew he was standing way too close to her to be friendly. His other hand settled on her lower back, cradling her waist in a way that erased any questions about his intentions. And then it trekked lower.

Rosie felt indignation burst like a geyser within her. How dare he make a pass at her, minutes after telling her how sweet *his Tammy* was? She felt her skin prickle and her brow furrow, wishing she had a mousetrap in her back pocket to reward him for his insolence!

A *snap!* echoed off the nearby trees, and Terry jumped away from her with a yelp.

"Ow! *Shit!*"

She turned, shocked, but not half as much as he was. He was holding his hand in front of him and then shook it out, staring at her wide-eyed but trying desperately not to look afraid.

"You shocked me," he said.

"Makes two of us," she said with a lifted chin, with much more confidence than she felt at that moment. She didn't know *what* had happened, but she was glad it had.

She turned away from the handsy woodsman, but then she froze. Her heart and shoulders sank as she recognized Tammy on her lawn, holding a foil-covered dish in front of her, just as frozen in place as Rosie was.

Terry must have seen her then, too, because his voice carried to her.

"Tammy!"

Tammy dropped the dish she was carrying and turned to hurry away at a light jog, but Terry, more athletic, caught up with her. They had an emphatic but quiet conversation while Rosie tried to look anywhere but at them. Terry glanced at her, and, not knowing what else to do, she retreated to the house.

She shifted the curtains in the front window to watch Terry hand Tammy into his pickup truck and then heard the truck start. She let the curtain fall back into place.

Poor Tammy.

CHAPTER FOUR

Rosie's third day of work started with her sleeping through her alarm. The mad rush to get Maggie ready to join her for her shift had her heart pumping. When they reached the Go-Go-Mart, Rosie knew she'd be fit in no time, what with all the walking she was doing each day.

Ben greeted her with a raised brow when they rushed in. They were five minutes early, but Rosie looked as guilty as someone who was fifteen minutes late. She'd promised him she was reliable, and she meant to keep her word.

"Hi," she said, dropping her bag under the counter. She undid her ponytail, shaking out her wild curls. The stiff morning breeze had whipped them up into a frenzy. She smoothed them back against her head to tame them.

"Hey," Ben said, glancing up from restocking the

magazine rack. "Nice quiet morning? Hi there, Maggie."

Maggie smiled and waved, holding her well-read copy of *Black Beauty*. Rosie smiled, finished tying her ponytail, and pulled the hair at the top to tighten the elastic. "Super relaxing," she quipped.

Ben nodded. "You're on the register today—think you can handle it?"

"Sure!" Rosie glanced at the cash register, as though they were already old friends. She'd worked a part-time job in retail when she'd first moved in with Randy, but that had been years ago. "It's like riding a bike," she said, trying to convince herself as she ran her fingertips across the keys.

"Okay," Ben said, raising a brow. "I'm gonna be stocking shelves—we're expecting a delivery today. You can sit in my office if you like, Maggie."

"Thanks!" Maggie said, thrilled not to be sitting up at the counter with her mom.

Ben grinned, holding out a hand to show Maggie where the door was before turning back to Rosie. "If you need me," he said, walking back towards the aisles, "just holler."

"Will do," Rosie agreed, switching on the old-timey radio that sat on a shelf behind the counter. Ben smiled and vanished into the depths of the store.

THE STORE WAS QUIET. REAL QUIET. SHE HADN'T expected Mosswood to be a thriving metropolis, but she had expected more than one customer. An older gentleman had wandered in and bought a copy of the local newspaper. After paying for it without speaking, he had snatched it off the counter and left. Rosie, shocked, was still wondering about him as she carried on with her duties. Were all the folks in town going to be so welcoming?

She hummed while she cleaned the counter, turning her attention to the shelves beside it. As she restocked chocolate bars and cough lozenges, Rosie couldn't help but feel as though the old man's reaction had been personal somehow. She finished adding gum to the display and stood, hearing the doors slide open behind her.

Great—fresh meat.

"Hi there, how's your—" Rosie trailed off when she turned and saw who had walked in. "—day?" she finished.

Prissy smirked, patting her hair into place.

"Why, Rosie." Prissy lifted her eyebrows and pressed her lips together in a thin line of clear disapproval. "Fancy seeing you here."

"Hi Prissy," Rosemary said, hyper-aware that she needed to be professional. "How are you?"

"Good, good..." Prissy looked around the store as though seeing it for the first time and not being sure she wanted to stay. "Need some staples, is all."

"Sure thing," Rosie said. "Plenty of staples to be had in here, that's for sure. Help yourself."

Prissy pulled a face before grabbing a wire shopping basket and heading into the first aisle. While Rosie hadn't expected genuine kindness or friendship from Prissy, the coldness in the other woman was off-putting. Rosie continued to tidy up the front counter area, but she could feel Prissy's eyes on her as she worked. Eventually, the other woman came up to the counter to finish her purchases. Rosie waited for her to place her items on the conveyer belt so that she could bag and check.

Prissy cleared her throat.

"Did you need something else, Priscilla?" Rosie glanced at the items in the basket. "We have cough lozenges over there by the mints."

Prissy raised an over-plucked brow. "Actually," she said with a predatory purr, "I'd like Ben to serve me if you don't mind."

What? Rosie blinked but recovered quickly.

"Ben's in back—we're expecting a delivery." She forced a smile. "I can help you, and then you won't need to wait."

"You don't get it, do you?" Prissy sighed as though dealing with moronic people was her daily cross to bear. "I want *Ben* to serve me because I don't want help from a classless home-wrecker."

At first, the words didn't register. Rosie stared as they sunk in, and then the incident with Terry came rushing to the forefront of her mind.

"Excuse me?" she asked, her voice so quiet it was almost a whisper.

"All the excuses in the world won't help a filthy harlot like you." Prissy smiled sweetly, but her words had the edge of a razor.

Rosie blinked. "Terry—"

"*Tammy's husband*," Prissy snapped, but Rosie ignored her.

"—came to my house yesterday afternoon under the pretense of helping me with yard work."

"He came over as a good Christian and a neighbor, and you couldn't help yourself, could you?" Prissy hissed. "He was shaking when he got home last night, the poor thing! And Tammy was beside herself! We had to hold an emergency prayer circle—"

"He *what?*" Rosie couldn't stop her voice from rising. "Is *that* the story he told y'all? He helped me shift a garden bench, and then he came onto me! Does that sound like being a good Christian or a good neighbor – or a decent husband—to you?"

Prissy rolled her eyes. "Do you really expect anyone to believe the words of a lying harlot over a trusted and respected member of this community?" She leaned forward then, her eyes glinting. "You made the biggest mistake of your life yesterday. I hope you can get out of your lease with Mrs. Wallace because you're *done* in this town."

Prissy straightened and smiled as though she hadn't just threatened Rosie's very existence in Mosswood.

"On second thought, I'll take my business elsewhere. Have a nice day." She set her basket on the counter and flounced out of the store.

By THE TIME THE AFTERNOON ROLLED AROUND, ROSIE was bored out of her brain. She'd had a total of three customers since lunch, and two of them gave her such stern looks as she served them that she wouldn't be surprised if they didn't come back. It looked like Terry's tale of woe at the hands of the new woman in town was spreading like wildfire. The bastard.

Ben had spent the afternoon in his office chatting to Maggie and shuffling through paperwork. He could do the task at night or at the counter between customers, and Rosie wondered if he needed her at all. Then she felt bad, hoping that her incident with Terry hadn't put people off shopping in the store.

She grabbed her bag, collected Maggie, saying goodbye to Ben before finishing her shift and ducking out of the store onto Main Street. The single cop car sat outside the Sheriff's Department across the road, and an elderly man sat on a bench outside the medical center next door to it. He waved to Rosie, and she smiled, waving back. That was the kind of good down-home feeling she was craving. But she wondered how long it would last, with Prissy and her posse on the warpath.

"Rosie Bell?!"

The voice was high-pitched, and the tone disbelieving. Rosie spun to see two women on the sidewalk directly in her path. She felt like a bucket of ice water had been dumped over her head.

The taller woman wore tight jeans, a black tank top, and black biker boots. The shorter woman was platinum blonde and wore a sour expression that matched her lemon-yellow pinup dress. They were chalk and cheese, and Rosie knew that better than anyone. Back in Atlanta, these women had been the sum of her circle of friends.

"Raquel, Mimi—hi," Rosie said cautiously, bringing Maggie close and pushing a smile onto her face. She was glad to see them but concerned about why they were two hours north of Atlanta in the tiny town she had escaped to from Randy.

"We wondered where on earth you'd got to," Mimi said, her concern for Rosie clear in her tone if not on her pinched face. "Especially when we tried your cell and got a disconnection message!"

Raquel was looking at her thoughtfully. "Randy just about turned the bar upside down, trying to shake information about you outta the place."

Rosie bit her lip, her eyes skipping down to Maggie and then back to the two women. She hesitated, wanting to lie—to pretend that she was skipping town in a matter of hours. Except now that she'd seen her friends, she wasn't so sure it would be a lie. How long before Randy got her location out of them?

"Magnolia," Rosie said, utilizing her 'Mom Said' tone, "why don't you skip on ahead to that bench down a ways and read a bit more of your book while I catch up with Racquel and Mimi?"

Maggie nodded, doing as she was told.

"Please don't tell him where I am," Rosie begged as soon as she thought her child was out of earshot. Raquel slipped her arm through Rosie's, moving them all down the sidewalk away from the doors of the Go-Go-Mart.

"Now don't you fret. We're only here to visit some little old dressmaker that Mimi here booked a fitting with. Ain't *nobody* knows you're here—ain't that right, Mimi?"

Mimi nodded. "We won't tell, Rosie. We promise."

"Fact is,' Raquel said, hugging Rosie's arm tighter. "You ain't done nothin' that the both of us ain't thought about doin' a hundred times or more. You always did have that fire in ya, Rosie."

Rosie relaxed a little, now that she knew she could count on her friends to keep her and Maggie off Randy's radar.

"I knew he would lose it," she murmured. "That sonofabitch didn't want me, except to be his maid. At least now he doesn't have to pretend to hide his sleepin' around." Rosie sighed. "I just feel bad for keepin' Maggie from her Daddy. Even such a one as him."

"Don't you worry about that now!" Mimi huffed. With a brood of kids herself, her maternal instincts were sharp. "He's been more butt-hurt about the indignity of you walkin' out on him than worryin' about his baby girl."

"Asshole," Rosie and Raquel said at the same time, and all three women laughed.

"I gotta go get Maggie," Rosie said, breaking contact with Raquel. She looked at her friends, feeling her heart growing heavier with each second that passed. "I'd invite y'all for dinner, but—"

"—but it's better that we don't know nothin' about nothin'," Raquel said matter-of-factly. She pressed a kiss to Rosie's cheek. "You go on now to your little one. And take care of yourself, Rosie."

"You too." Rosie gave them both a hug. "Both of you. If I can do it, so can you."

Her friends looked wistful as they let her go. And even though they had promised to keep her secret, Rosie dragged Maggie home at break-neck speed, looking over her shoulder the whole time.

CHAPTER FIVE

S aturday dawned with a promise that had Rosie whistling as she tidied the kitchen before breakfast. Sun streamed through the newly cleaned kitchen window that framed the perfect view of Mosswood nestled in the crook of the Chickasaw river. Rosie rested her hip on the side of the kitchen sink, drying the last few dishes from dinner the night before.

Having a job, earning her own money, and doing her own thing felt fantastic. But there was a Randy-shaped cloud floating over her head that was threatening to rain on her parade. She didn't think that Raquel and Mimi would rat her out, but she knew how persistent Randy could be when he wanted something. Once upon a time, it had been her.

But she couldn't afford to live her life the same way she did when they had been under the same roof. Rosie had sworn to herself in the long, anxiety-inducing cab ride to Mosswood that she would never be controlled by another man as long as she lived, and she'd meant it. She had to set a good example for Maggie and teach her that life was more than doing what other people wanted you to do.

As if on cue, two tiny arms slipped around her waist from behind. Smiling, Rosie turned as far as she could to wrap an arm around her daughter's shoulders.

"Morning, Pumpkin." She pressed a kiss to the top of Maggie's messy-haired head.

"Morning."

It always amused Rosie how cranky Maggie sounded in the mornings. She was always up and at it early, usually before the sun was up. It was a cheat's way of feeling like more could fit into one day, and it was a trick that Rosie had learned early on during her career as a mother.

"How'd you sleep?"

Maggie shrugged, burying her face into Rosie's fluffy, bright teal dressing gown. It had daisies printed on all over it and had been a gift for her birthday last year. "Weird dreams," Maggie muttered at last.

"About?"

"Doesn't matter."

Rosie frowned slightly, pursing her lips. It wasn't very often that Maggie didn't want to share something with her. She knew that up and leaving Atlanta and Randy had been a big deal for them both and hoped Maggie was coping okay. Rosie remembered what they had been talking about a few days before while pulling weeds, and an idea popped into her head.

"You know what? Why don't we get dressed and go explore the town? We can get something for breakfast while we're out. Have a look at the river. Maybe there's ducks!"

She heard Maggie's excited gasp even before her daughter pulled back to look into her face.

"Really, Mom?"

"Really-really!" Rosie grinned, her heart swelling. She would do just about anything to see that look of bright enthusiasm on her child's face. "Go get dressed— I'll race you!"

"No FAIR, YOU'VE GOT LONGER LEGS THAN I DO!"

Rosie laughed as she and Maggie climbed higher on the tall pyramid-style high ropes course. They had both been super excited to discover the playground right next to the river in town. Though Maggie was getting to be a little too old for most of the playground equipment there, the pyramid had sparked joy.

"Yeah, well, you're quicker'n I am," Rosie tossed back, grinning as she hoisted herself higher. "You should have been at the top already!"

"I don't want to beat you too bad," Maggie called. "I don't wanna make you feel old."

Great. Thanks. Rosie shook her head with a rueful

laugh as she followed after her daughter. Maggie took after her side, she decided, even though she didn't know what that might entail. Being in foster care meant that her side of the old family tree was pretty bare. But she'd met Randy's parents, and she knew for a fact that her sweet girl didn't keep any of their traits.

"Mom!" Maggie stopped climbing and huffed. "C'mon, you're not even moving!"

"Right," Rosie reached for the highest rope she could grab, looking to make up for lost time in more ways than one. She made it to the very tip of the pyramid only a couple of seconds after Maggie. The pair of them shared a hug as they looked out over what they could see of Mosswood. A gentle breeze took hold of a loose lock of Maggie's dark hair, fluttering it underneath Rosie's nose. She smiled and bent close to her daughter's ear.

"Last one down's a rotten egg," she whispered.

Rosie was more calculated and less robust as she made her way back down the laddered ropes of the pyramid. Maggie made it to the ground fast, moving on to other playground equipment while she waited for her mom. As Rosie got close enough to the ground to jump, she grabbed a lower rope and swung, letting go at what she judged to be the right moment. She landed on the soft sand below the pyramid awkwardly. Her hands shot back up to find a rope to hold onto as she overbalanced, but they found solid flesh instead.

Declan looked down into her face, his characteristic

swagger momentarily masked with concern. "Whoa there," he said softly. "Are ya alright?"

Her hands had perched themselves on the solid curves of his biceps. She could feel the warmth of his skin through his grey polo shirt. He was so tall she had to crane her neck to look up into his face, which was inches from hers as he inspected her expression for signs of pain.

"Thanks," she said, tucking a lock of hair behind her ear.

Maggie gave up on her swing and wandered over. In a move worthy of a comedy act, both adults straightened and attempted to look benevolent. She glanced between them, her eyes narrowing in an expression that said she wasn't buying any of it.

"Mom, can we get ice cream?" she asked, pushing boundaries while she thought her mother's resolve might be a little weaker. "There's a shop right over there." She pointed with her chin to a row of stores lining the riverfront.

Rosie's heart sank. There was absolutely no way her loose change could stretch to buying non-essential ice cream, and Ben had already told her that she'd get her first check on Tuesday... three whole days away. She'd been too ashamed to ask him for an advance. Rosie had already adopted an apologetic air as she started to respond, but Declan grinned at Maggie.

"Abso-fu-*ahh*-lutely," he said, canceling out the curse word upon a sharp glare from Rosie.

"Awesome!" Maggie crowed as she ran on ahead, leaving Rosie to walk with Declan. "This is kind of you," she admitted as they walked along the riverfront, "but it's not necessary. We've never had a lot of money, so she's good about having to wait for special occasions."

The day was melting into one of those afternoons prepped for a stunning sunset. The grass on the banks of the river was short until the water's edge, where it grew a little wild. Ducks quacked soft hellos as Rosie and Declan trailed along behind Maggie.

A strange shadow passed over Declan's face. The arrogance he usually wore like a custom leather jacket was gone. "Buying you ice cream is the least I can do," he said, shoving his huge hands into the pockets of his blue jeans.

Rosie frowned. "You don't have to do anything," she insisted.

"You're my Queen," he told her, as though saying that was the most natural thing in the world. "There's nothing I wouldn't do for you."

She had to give him points for sticking with his story. And for persistence.

"Still with the Queen of the witches thing?" Rosie side-eyed him. "Really?"

"Witch Queen," he corrected her, "accordin' to royal protocols. And yes? It's not as though I made it up to get in your pants."

A laugh threatened to escape her. It had been a long

time since any man—including Randy—had wanted to get into her pants. The fact that two men had tried it since she had come to town made her question the safety of the town's water supply.

"That's exactly what someone who had made it up to get in my pants would say," she declared.

A knowing smirk caught hold of his lips, tempting her eyes to linger there a little longer than they should. With his beard and broad shoulders, he looked like a sexy lumberjack fresh out of some woodland grove.

Straight Outta Killarney.

Maggie skipped through the door of Fortescue's Ice Cream Emporium with an enthusiasm that made Rosie smile. Declan stepped ahead of her to get the door, holding it open and standing to the side so she could pass through. He smiled at her as he waited for her to pass by.

"M'lady," he murmured with the slightest dip of his head as she stepped through the doorway.

Maggie had insisted on sitting next to Declan, tucking into her Banana Bonanza sundae. Rosie settled for a cup of black coffee. She sipped at it more because it gave her something to do rather than out of any real need for caffeine.

Declan chatted with Maggie, answering countless questions about his funny accent, Ireland, and about why he was so tall. He licked his plain vanilla ice cream, all traces of his arrogance and self-important swagger blanketed by an effortless charm.

"Are there actually leprechauns in Ireland?" Maggie asked before digging out another spoonful of sundae. "Like, for real?"

He chuckled. "Well, now I don't know anythin' 'bout no leprechauns." He sank back against the powder blue vinyl seat of the booth they were in. "But I can tell ya that Ireland is full t'the brim with witches."

Rosie met his gaze over the brim of her coffee cup, her eyes narrowing. If he started the witch-talk with Maggie, she would put the brakes on this outing so fast he'd get whiplash.

"I don't like witches," Maggie complained, showing her cherry to the side of her plate with her spoon. "They're scary."

"Some witches *are* scary," he agreed, nodding his head in deference to Rosie. He reached for the cherry stalk, plucking it from the bowl. Rosie's annoyance at the witch talk flared into dismay over the loss of those empty Maraschino calories. "But most of them are good people."

He held the cherry out across the table by the stalk, jiggling it at Rosie. She glanced at it, then back to him.

Later that night, when replayed the day in her mind, she would think about that moment. The sensation as she took the cherry from the Irishman would come back to her as a spreading heat. Little sparks of warmth jumped from his fingertips to hers, leaving an impression that would affect her for hours afterward.

Declan smirked.

Maggie hadn't even looked up from stirring her ice cream into banana-flavored soup. "Do you know some witches?" she asked, mystified.

"I've met my fair share," he teased.

"Cool!"

Declan grinned. "See?" he told Rosie. "Your wee'an thinks I'm cool."

"She's ten," Rosie countered with sass, "and you bought her ice cream."

He glanced back at Maggie, narrowing his eyes with false suspicion. "Ten?! I thought she was twenty!" he exclaimed with a gasp that made her dissolve into giggles.

IT TOOK ROSIE A FULL TWO HOURS AFTER MAGGIE HAD fallen asleep to be able to relax. She lost count of how many times she had peered out of the living room window at the gravel drive leading to the house. When she was finally sure that there wasn't going to be a sexy Irishman unexpectedly knocking on her door, she decided to chill. Rather than sitting on the porch with her wine tonight, she locked up the house and ran herself a bath.

The old claw foot tub was huge, and the warm, sudsy water enveloped her like a hug. Steam swirled into the air, driven by a light breeze that came through the bathroom window. The candle she had lit flickered playfully. The day melted away, and Rosie allowed her mind to wander from worries and on to other things.

Surprisingly, her mind settled on men. It had been twenty-two years since she had been single, and at least twenty since Randy had started policing where her eyes lingered. It had been a long damn time since she'd had a man make her feel... well—anything, other than revulsion. So, alone in her bathtub, she allowed her thoughts to go where they willed.

Like to the dimple in Ben's left cheek when he had smiled at her that afternoon. Ben was cinnamon-spiced apple pie, with a generous serving of cream. Comforting, clean-cut. Wholesome.

If Ben was apple pie, then Randy was wilted bitter greens. Hard to swallow, and no matter how much you tolerated, it didn't ever seem like there was less of it on your plate.

Declan was something else altogether. She replayed the way he'd swooped her up in his arms like she was as light as a dried leaf. She remembered the strength in his grip when he'd held her on the playground. He was full-bodied whiskey, with a hint of chili powder.

A deep exhale escaped her at the thought. She slid her hands over her abdomen, suds skimming down her legs as the candlelight cast enchanting shadows across the scene.

And then she was in the dark.

Rosie froze before realizing that the breeze must have snuffed out her candle. She sighed into the darkness, not wanting to break the spell she had been under and get out of the bath yet.

She explored her body like it was a city she'd once known well but had lost her way in recently. Strangely, her touch didn't feel like her own touch. Her hands felt somehow larger and rougher, even though that was impossible. Her mind focused on a crooked smile, smoky jade green eyes, and a head of shaggy ginger hair that she longed to pull.

When her release came, she felt like she was coming alive again. All the tension of the past few years—leaving Randy, worrying for her daughter and herself—melted into a mellowness that she'd never known. She sighed again, but it was a lighter and more contented sound than before. Rosie ran her hands through the cooling water and then up over her face. The sensation was liberating, and she felt more like herself than she had for decades.

And when Rosie opened her eyes, the candle was burning once more.

CHAPTER SIX

Two days later, Rosie and Maggie made their way down Main Street again for her morning shift at the Go-Go-Mart. The weekend had passed in a haze of DIY projects, and the cottage was looking much more hospitable. The living room had been thoroughly dust-busted, and the freshly washed drapes were a pretty shade of cornflower blue, not the murky grey Rosie had first assumed them to be. The couch was going to prove a more worthy adversary, but Rosie was confident she would be able to hire a steam cleaner from somewhere.

Because tomorrow, Tuesday, she would have actual money in her pocket. The kind that she'd earned herself and hadn't had to coax out of a controlling ex-husband. She chirped a greeting to Ben as she slung her bag under the counter, pausing to scoop her long, chocolate brown hair up into a high ponytail that accentuated her bangs.

"Oh, hi Rosie, Maggie," Ben said, appearing from the office. He approached the counter with a glance in Maggie's direction. "Did y'all have a good weekend?"

Rosie smiled, tightened her hair tie, and glanced at the box of unpacked gum waiting for her on the counter. "We did! You?"

"Well, I worked, so..." Ben shrugged. There was a strange catch in his voice, and he was beating around a bush of some kind.

Rosie quirked a brow. "Everything okay?"

Ben took a deep breath and let it out before speaking again. "Maggie? Would you like to read in my office again?"

Maggie nodded. "Yes, please."

He waited for her to pass through the door into the office but kept his voice low as though he had way too much personal experience with eavesdropping children. "I know that you have a family life, Rosie," he began, "but I'd rather you didn't bring personal issues to work."

She froze, her good mood vanished, and her smile fizzed out in its wake. "What do you mean? I don't have any personal—"

"Your husband called here yesterday," Ben interjected. "Something about you were meant to get your daughter back to him for the weekend, and you didn't show."

Rosie froze. Ben continued talking, but his words barely registered. She couldn't hear them anyway over the ringing in her ears. Her chest felt tight and full, and she couldn't catch her breath even though she knew she was breathing.

"Okay?" Ben finished. Even though she had no idea what he had said, Rosie nodded. She pulled the box of gum closer to her and began to draw the foil-wrapped packages out in a daze.

She got paid tomorrow. She could ask Ben to cash it for her since she didn't have a bank account yet. That was believable. Then she could hire a cab, or steal Declan's truck. They had enough food to eat for a few towns anyway. They could drive until his gas ran out, and then they could walk.

"Rosie?"

Ben's voice interrupted her planning, and she realized that she was shoving piles of gum into a chocolate bar spot. She hurriedly pulled them back out onto the counter.

"Sorry, Ben," she felt herself murmuring. "It won't happen again."

THE TRICKLE OF CUSTOMERS THINNED TO A HALT BEFORE lunch. It seemed like a good time to get a jump on restocking. Rosie went to the front door of the store and did a quick survey of the street—quiet as usual—before stepping out of the back door and into the loading dock area.

The loading dock was just a big concrete porch with no railings so that delivery trucks could pull right up alongside it and unload. A stack of battered-looking crates filled the right corner of the dock, leaning haphazardly against the store's brick wall. An old armchair was nearby, and Rosie guessed that this was the unofficial Go-Go-Mart break room. A tin roof extended over the area so that it was out of the weather.

She shuffled towards the neatly piled cardboard boxes on the left of the dock and lifted one box of soda cans. It was heavy, but physical work always made her feel better. She supposed it was the endorphins. After hefting it to the counter inside, Rosie turned and made her way back out to the dock to grab a carton of diet soda as well.

Declan's truck was parked alongside the dock. He came around the truck to the ladder that allowed access to the asphalt in the alley. He glanced up at her as he climbed.

"Mornin'," he grinned lazily, turning to step onto the bed of the pickup where wooden cartons waited to be unloaded.

"Hey," she responded, half in her thoughts.

"Let me take those," Declan said, removing the case of diet soda from her arms. She let him and stayed on the porch long after he left. She felt far away, staring at the beat-up old truck that he had parked by the loading dock.

"You keep starin' at her like that," said Declan as he

came back for another load, "and I'm gonna think you like my truck more than me!"

Rosie felt tears threatening to overcome her for the second time that morning. She refused to give in to them. She lashed out with her leg instead, kicking one of the empty wooden crates. The whole stack tumbled down onto the loading dock.

Declan's brows lifted as he watched her episode, his eyes wide. He was by her side in a heartbeat, even though it was clear that he had no idea what to do with the situation.

"Hey," he finally said in a soft tone, placing a beefy hand on her shoulder as he guided her towards the chair. "What's goin' on?"

"Nothing," she huffed, knowing how stupid she sounded as soon as the words had left her mouth.

Declan tilted his head to the side, eyeing her as though she were a horse that might bolt at the first chance it had. He wasn't far off. "Don't sound like nothin'," he prompted. "I can't help ya fix what I don't know is broken, love."

"Stop calling me stupid pet names," she snapped. "It's not your problem to fix. And even if it *was*, you wouldn't be able to do anything about it anyway."

"I know from experience, darlin'," he said, ignoring her command. "And this is *somethin'*, not nothin'. And ignorin' it ain't gonna do a damn thing."

To hear perfect sense coming from a man who still maintained that she was the queen of all witches was

79

jarring. Rosie blinked up at him and took a deep, shaky breath.

As though he could sense that the storm had passed, he squatted next to her chair. He was so tall that even like this, he was nearly eye-level with her. "Let me guess," he said ruefully. "It's a problem with a fella."

She let the breath out and shook her head. Her tears came in a flood. "Not just a *fella*. A… *demon*." She looked through the veil of blurring tears and into his gaze, and the words tumbled out. "My ex. Randy."

Now that she was on the precipice of telling someone about what had happened, Rosie wasn't sure she wanted to make the leap. What did it say about her that she spent all that time letting herself get run down? What kind of mother was she to not have made the break sooner? Her hands started to shake, and she grabbed the hem of her Go-Go-Mart polo shirt in her fists to stop them.

"You're alright," Declan said softly, sliding forward onto his knees as he realized this was going to be a longer conversation than either of them had bargained for. She took in what she hoped would be a bolstering gulp of air. He reached forward to untangle one of her hands so that he could envelop it in his. "You're alright," he repeated. "You don't have to talk about this if ya don't wanna," ducking his head to meet her gaze, "but I'm here t'listen if ya do."

Perhaps it was the sincerity she could read in his usually cheeky eyes. Maybe it was the crushing weight of carrying around the baggage – all those years of putting up with what she assumed was her lot. Dreaming of better but not believing that she *deserved* better. But whatever the reason, Rosie felt the story start pouring out with her tears.

"I'd been with Randy since I was seventeen," she began, looking down at their hands entwined. "Since I was a kid. I had lived in the foster care system my whole life—" she scoffed, and then corrected herself. "Well, *survived* is probably a better way to describe it. Anyway, by the time I had made it through high school, I was a nobody. I wasn't rich enough to be fashionable, not fashionable enough to be popular, and not popular enough to be noticed – except by Randy."

He squeezed her hand. Her lips twitched to smile at the gesture, but she was too lost in her memories. "*He* made me feel like *somebody* – at least in the beginning. He was older and had a motorcycle. Most of the girls in my senior year swooned whenever they spotted him around town. They couldn't believe it when he seemed interested in little ol' me."

In her mind, she could see it all like it was yesterday. The gas-station flowers she'd been so impressed by— the promises of protection, loyalty, *love*. Looking back now, she could see how Randy might have thought he was in love. But love didn't let people do the things he'd done to her and Maggie.

"I couldn't believe it, either," she admitted. It felt so foolish now, and she hated herself for having thought that a man could be the glue that would hold the shattered fragments of her life together. "Nothin' was too much trouble. And he was always complimenting me, tellin' me things like..." she trailed off, as though she didn't want to go back to that place where Randy had made her feel anything good. "Don't matter now, I suppose. What I didn't know was that he was an up-and-comer with the Marauders biker gang."

Declan bit his bottom lip, as though he wanted to say something but was determined to listen.

"Any mean streak he'd had in him all along grew wider once he started up with the Marauders," Rosie told him, brushing a stream of tears away. "They all treated their women like possessions, and he was desperate to fit in. We'd go back and forth, a few months as a normal couple. Him comin' home for dinner, then a few months of him bein' what they wanted him to be. By the time I realized he was never gonna change, it was too late. I was twenty-nine years old and pregnant with a baby I was desperate to keep."

"Maggie," Declan said.

"Maggie," Rosie confirmed, unable to keep a sad smile from her face at the mention of her daughter. "Guess somewhere deep down, I thought that havin' someone else to love would make up for the love I didn't already have."

He watched her face intently. "Did it work?"

"A bit," she admitted. "But mostly, it helped me

realize that my love for her was bigger than my fear of him."

"So, you left."

"So, I left."

"And now he's comin' after ya."

She nodded. "He knows where I am." She dug the phone she had purchased from the Go-Go Mart out of her back pocket and checked it, worried he might have somehow traced her through it. The screen was blank. Pressing her lips together, she lifted her free hand to sweep her bangs to the side as though it might help her to see the situation more clearly. "It's only a matter of time before he shows up."

"Well," Declan huffed with a determined look in his eyes. "I *could* sort it out for ya right quick enough," he told her with another squeeze of her hand, "but that'd be doin' you no good. What you need is to be able to protect yourself and Maggie."

Rosie's gaze danced over his face, looking for clues that he was making fun of her. Finding none, she discovered that she was grateful for his advice.

"And how do I do that?" she sighed, closing her eyes for a moment. A moment later, warmth blanketed her cheek. She opened her eyes to find Declan's hand gently cupping her face, the pad of his thumb brushing her skin. She could see a light dusting of freckles across his large nose, as though the connection had thrown everything into high definition.

"Don't run," he said, meeting her gaze. She felt her

breath catch in her chest to be caught out, but she listened as he swiped his thumb across her cheek. "You got more people on your team here in Mosswood than you realize. I'm one of 'em."

He reached for the phone in her hand and began typing into it. She felt a fleeting moment of panic. He would have just seen that the only contacts in her phone were Ben, Mosswood Elementary, and Carol-Ann from Wallace Realty. How embarrassing.

"There. Now I'm in your contacts. If there's any trouble, or ya need *anythin'*, you call me."

She looked up at him as he stood, their hands disconnecting. "Thanks, Declan," she breathed. She sniffled as she stood with him. Even though her problem was still very much a problem, somehow, her head felt a lot clearer about it all. "I really appreciate it."

"No worries," he smiled, slipping his hands into his pockets. "Think about getting' some kinda security," he told her. "Better to be prepared, come what may. Bit harder for problems to *be* problems when they can't get at ya."

A light frown creased Rosie's brow. "Right," she sighed. "Security." How much was *that* going to cost her?

But how much was it going to cost her if she didn't do something about Randy?

LATER THAT NIGHT, WITH MAGGIE TUCKED IN BED AND sound asleep, Rosie sat on a stool at her kitchen counter, researching home security systems on her phone. They were all expensive. She'd have to find a company in a nearby town because there were zero providers in Mosswood. There were smart home options, of course, but as far as she could tell, Fox Cottage didn't even have a phone line, much less high-speed internet.

She closed the browser tab of a company that wanted to charge an annual fee. It was time to change up her search parameters. 'Home protection' seemed like the next logical step from 'home security,' right?

Search results flooded the phone screen. She flicked through them, noticing one result was a little different from the others.

'Protecting your Home: Modern Hearth Magic.'

Hearth magic? What on earth was that? There was no other preview text to give her a clue, and after a moment, Rosie's curiosity got the better of her. She clicked the link, and a bright purple website sprung to life on the screen.

'Concerned with negative energy in your life? Worried about unwanted people bringing their bad juju whenever they visit? Read on for 13 hot tips on how to use hearth magic to protect your kith and kin...'

With a skeptical brow raised, Rosie read on through the article. It mentioned things like rock salt, moon water, crystals, and sprigs of rosemary. *Ironic.* She thought about the strange incidents she'd experienced since arriving in Mosswood, even before Declan had insisted that there was more to her than she knew. She didn't really think she was a witch, though, did she?

If she had some of the ingredients mentioned in the article, she could put her growing doubts about her alleged magical ability to rest once and for all.

Rosie managed to round up the rock salt from the pantry and a small piece of quartz from Maggie's rock collection. A rosemary bush grew at the end of the driveway. The only thing she wouldn't have would be moon water, whatever that was, so she would have to make do without it. She took the herb back inside and got to work, following the instructions in the article to the letter. She soon had a small bundle tied up neatly in a piece of paper towel. The recipe—if that's what witches called them—had called for cheesecloth, but she didn't have any. She was certain that the charm wouldn't work anyway, so it hardly mattered.

The recipe said to cast the spell at midnight. Rosie took her charm and the carton of salt and set them down by the front door, preparing herself for the next step. She had half considered ignoring it, but it was supposedly the most important part. She took a deep breath and stripped out of her daily jeans-and-tee combo until she was completely nude. And then she picked up her ingredients and stepped out onto the porch.

The charm was to go in the mailbox, which was at the end of the driveway, so she decided to do that bit last. While it was unlikely that anyone would be driving through the woods in the middle of the night, Rosie needed to build a little confidence first. She began on the porch, tipping the carton of salt so that a thin trickle poured on the ground. She tried to remember the chant, kicking herself for not having written it down.

> *"Mother Moon, please hear my call*
> *Let your light upon me fall*
> *Shine your shield upon my home*
> *And follow me elsewhere I roam*
> *Charge with power this simple charm*
> *Guard against those who mean harm…"*

SHE CONTINUED THE INCANTATION, DOING A WIDE circle around the perimeter of her home. She reached the mailbox at last and popped the charm into it.

> *"By earth and flame and wind and sea*
> *As I pray so may it be."*

A gentle breeze sprung up into the tops of the oak

trees surrounding the house like a whisper of approval. The Spanish moss drifted in slow-moving waves. Rosie was so distracted by its beauty she forgot she was standing stark naked on the side of the road. And then she heard a branch snap in the brush right across from her.

She froze, not knowing whether to scream or bolt. Everything was silent until a rustling sound, and moving bushes proved that she was not imagining things. Rosie opened her mouth, but her voice caught in the back of her throat. She took a large gulp of air and was about to scream when a creature snuck out of the woods.

Almost entirely white except for its black head and paws, she almost mistook it for a small dog or cat. That was, until the black face and white stripe gave it away for what it really was: a skunk. It peered at her lazily, black eyes full and child-like in the moonlight. She slipped one arm protectively across her boobs to hide them from its inquisitive gaze, her other hand dropping to cover her lady parts, Eve style.

"Shoo!" she called to the creature, but it took no notice of her. It merely waddled forward across her path, until two small kits caught up to her. They all turned to stare at her, mama and her two babes.

"Er—" she began, unsure of the situation. "Um… good skunks? I'ma… erm… just… gah!"

She took off running down the driveway, her long brown hair streaming behind her and the whiteness of her retreating form pale and ghostlike in the moonlight.

She didn't stop running until she was on the porch, and she looked back towards the road as she tried to catch her breath.

The skunk family was nowhere in sight, and Rosie ran over the incident in her mind. She took a long, steadying breath and leaned one hand on the porch railing. Surveying her front yard, Rosie remembered why she was out there in the first place. With a glance up at the sky, which held a fat moon but not a full one, she shrugged.

"Blessed be!" She said to no one in particular, before turning to take proper cover in the house.

CHAPTER SEVEN

Rosie wasn't sure that her hearth magic had even worked, but by the time she had crawled into bed, she was exhausted. The whirlwind of events since she and Maggie had left Atlanta had wrung her out and left her to dry. She fell into a deep sleep with strange dreams hovering on the edges of her consciousness.

She could pick out the sweet, round face of Tammy Holt, but the cheerful-seeming woman looked full of a sorrow that made Rosie ache. An egg hit Tammy on the side of the face, causing a deep purple bruise to spread across her eye socket and cheekbone like dark ink. The scene spun, blurring. Rosie watched it become a scene where Carol-Ann Wallace was sitting at a desk in her realtor office, reaching out to stroke a huge kangaroo that twitched its ears in response. And then there was Maggie, chocolate ice cream spread over her face, sitting on an old tire swing. 'Mom?' she called, each time the swing brought her towards Rosie. 'Mom?'

"Mom?"

Rosie jolted awake, just in time to hear what sounded like an explosion and shouting out in the woods. The explosion caused a window somewhere in the house to shatter. Maggie shrieked from where she had been hovering in the doorway. Rosie gasped and leaped to her feet beside the bed.

"I'm here, Pumpkin," she breathed, rushing to Maggie's side. She pulled her close while straining her ears to hear what was going on. She pressed a rushed kiss to the top of her daughter's head.

"Stay still, okay?" Maggie nodded as Rosie crept to the bedroom window, peeling back the curtains. She looked out across the dark expanse of lawn that led to the cottage.

A dull sooty glow lit up the woods beyond the drive, complete with a mass of smoke that rose into the pitch-dark sky. A chill came over Rosie as she watched the fire increase with intensity before her very eyes. She was shocked as several thoughts crowded her mind all at once. Was it a forest fire? The shouts she could still hear didn't sound like the commands of a fire-fighting crew; they sounded angry. And then she realized that the fire was in the same clearing where Declan's camper was.

Holy shit.

"Stay here," she barked at Maggie, dashing past her to yank on her sneakers. "Lock the front door after me and get under my bed. Do not come out until I tell you to, okay?"

"I wanna come with you!" Maggie protested, eyes wide.

Rosie did up her second shoelace, straightened, and moved to place her hands on Maggie's' little shoulders. "Declan is in trouble, and I gotta go help him out. You need to stay here. I need you to do something important, okay?" She turned, snatching her phone from her bedside table before pressing it into Maggie's hands. "I need you to get under the bed and then dial 9-1-1. Stay on the phone with them. Tell them our address, that there's a fire and that there may be people hurt. Can you do that?"

Swallowing nervously, Maggie nodded.

"Good girl," Rosie said approvingly, and then took off.

As soon as she was out of the cottage, the smell of smoke was thick in the air. There were a few more shouts, and she doubled her efforts to get across the lawn in record time. As she got closer to the clearing, bits of ash drifted through the air, clouding her vision. She coughed as she ran, desperate to breathe in more oxygen and less smoke. She wished she had stopped to get something to cover her mouth with, but she hadn't thought that far ahead, so she pulled the neck of her t-shirt up instead.

The clearing was close now. She heard a strange whooshing sound as she approached; the shouting stopped. As she burst through the trees, she felt the heat of the fire rush up to her skin. And then Rosie heard a sound that made her feel like being sick.

A throng of engines started not too far away; the low, throaty growl of motorcycles. They revved a few times, and then she heard them peel away, leaving her in no doubt about who had instigated this attack.

The whooshing noise distracted her from looking in the direction of the motorcycle engines. It was only then that she saw Declan.

He stood right in the face of the fire. He was silhou-etted against the raging flames that completely engulfed his camper. His feet were planted wide, his arms raised in defiance of the destruction raging before his eyes. The whoosh came from jets of water streaming right out of Declan's palms, as forceful as the stream from any fire-truck hose. Rosie watched, transfixed, as he angled his powerful shoulders from left to right and back again, focusing the water on different parts of the fire.

There is no possible explanation for this, she thought. There is no real way he could just be shooting water out of his hands like canons.

She had been holding her breath, partly in shock and partly to avoid breathing in the smoke. Now that she was ready to inhale, the contaminated air caught in the back of her seared throat and made her start coughing. Declan turned. One jet of water vanished as though he might be ready to create a little fire of his own for anyone stupid enough to get in his way. When he saw it was Rosie, concern flooded his face, and the other jet ceased as well.

"What're ya doin' here?" he called to her. His long strides made short work of the ground between them as he crossed immediately to her side.

She coughed some more, bending double and resting her hands on her knees. He patted her on the back, gently at first and then more firmly in a bid to help her coughing. When she straightened, she noticed that the water had worked. The flames that still licked the insides of the camper were small, even though the outside was black.

"You," she tried, and coughed again as she straightened.

"I'm fine," he said quickly, pleased that she was concerned enough for his welfare to come bolting through the woods in the middle of the night to get to him in his hour of need. He shifted to slide an arm around her shoulders, meaning to draw her into him.

Rosie shrugged him off, taking a step back. "You— can do—magic!" she wheezed, her eyes wide.

Declan held his arms out, pretending to be hurt that she didn't seem to want to fall into his well-muscled embrace like a damsel in distress. But he couldn't hold the expression for long. Telltale crinkles appeared at the corners of his eyes, and before long, he fixed her with a slow, smooth grin.

"Look, I've been tellin' you I'm a Witch King for a while now. S'not my fault ya don't listen."

She watched him for a while, ignoring his amusement at her 'sudden revelation' in favor of looking for something deeper. Understanding, perhaps? Her eyes flicked over his expression. When she finally came up empty-handed, she swallowed the foul taste in her mouth—whether it was ash or embarrassment remained to be seen. She didn't like being made fun of for something that she couldn't even fathom.

"A drunken stranger who sounds like the poster boy for Lucky Charms throws himself into my life, telling me that not only is magic real but that I can do it because I'm a Witch Queen." Her voice dripped with sarcasm that was only mildly hindered by the smoke-infused husk in her tone. "And for some reason, it surprises you that I thought until three minutes ago that you were a total whack-job?"

Declan huffed a chuckle through his nose. He glanced away as though trying to make sure their invisible audience wasn't paying attention and then leaned towards her.

"You can play with my Lucky Charms any time you like," he grinned, unable to hide his amusement at his own joke.

"Ugh!" Rosie replied, throwing up her hands and turning on her heel. "I have to get back to a terrified child who is hiding under my bed, calling the authorities. Thanks for your delightful company," she threw over her shoulder.

"Wait—she what now?" The aura of mirth

surrounding him poofed into non-existence as he scurried after her, the flames behind them lessening with each passing second.

"Fire department," Rosie stated, ticking off a finger. "Sheriff's department," another tick, "paramedics. You name it, I told her to call them. And she'd have done it properly, too. She's watched enough You-Tube videos of kids who saved their parents' lives, Lord knows it!"

Declan muttered something under his breath. He paused and then rushed to catch up with Rosie again as she carved a path through the woods towards Fox Cottage.

"You're sure about this? I don't wanna put ya out."

The medium-sized living room at Fox Cottage seemed small and crowded when there was a tall, strapping Irishman filling it. Rosie shook out the spare linens she had painstakingly laundered at the Kwik Kleen. She glanced at him as he looked around the room.

She didn't have money to get any knick-knacks, so the room was bare aside from what had been there when they moved in. An ancient floor lamp that looked like it was made in 1969 sat in the corner. An age-pitted mirror hung above the fireplace. A tiny TV that still had bunny-ear antennae was in pride of place.

And there, along the main wall, was the couch. It

was perfectly serviceable, and Rosie loved the way it afforded her a pretty view of the front garden. The scene was visible through the net curtains in the large bay window that was begging for a window-seat to be installed.

But now that they were there setting Declan up for his first night of couch-surfing, she could see why he was hesitant. He was at least two feet too long for the couch for starters, and at least a foot too wide for it. It was lumpy on account of it being older than she was. Although she had cleaned it thoroughly, it was a weird mottled cream color covered with a pattern of strange green flowers. Rosie adored it, but she got why it might seem less than appealing.

The only reason Declan was even there was because she felt responsible for him now having nowhere to live.

"You're not putting me out," she repeated as she made the couch up for him. "It's the least I can do."

He peered at her curiously over his shoulder. "Aye?"

"Well, you've helped me out a few times now. In my mind, that makes us friends." She tucked a lock of hair behind her ear. "And I'd like to help a friend if they needed me to."

A few moments of silence settled between them. She almost regretted being so forthright in her estimation of him as a 'friend.' He shuffled a foot on the carpet, turning as if to take in the rest of the room. When his eyes came to rest on the fireplace, he appeared to find the change of topic he seemed to be looking for.

"Does this thing work?" He had crawled halfway into the fireplace and was squinting up the chimney. "I think it needs cleanin'."

"Well, I'm sure there's lots of things that need doing around the place," Rosie said with false cheer. She fluffed the pillow she had commandeered for him from her own bed. "You'll be able to get stuck in and lend a hand."

She could hear his light chuckle drift up the flue, and she smirked as she finished setting up his makeshift bed. He joined her, plopping onto the couch and upsetting all the hard work she had done. She gave him A Look ™, but he patted the sofa next to him, suggesting she sit down.

"It's late," she said.

"Doubt I'll be sleepin' much tonight anyway," he said, and her guilt sprang up enough to be coaxed by his patting the couch again. She took a seat clear on the other side of the sofa.

"So." Rosie could feel her heart pick up a beat just thinking about it. "What happened?"

"Your ex's mates, I imagine." Declan sniffed and leaned back on the couch. "They rocked up and brought me some Molotov cocktails to get the party started. Luckily, I was able to get out through the back window." He brushed his thumb across the shorn beard on his throat. "Not too clever, that lot. Thank fuck."

She shook her head. "I'm so sorry you got caught up in all this."

He leaned closer to her. "Hey," he said, trying to get her to look up at him. "I was already caught up in all this." He shook his head and sighed. "We need to get ya some security sorted out."

She bristled, leaping up from the couch. "I tried! I was up for hours last night looking at security systems that I can't afford and security companies that don't even service Mosswood—if I could afford those, that is. I even—" she trailed off and decided to start again. "I'm not sure what you expect me to do, exactly, on the salary I'm earning."

"You even what?"

Realizing her mistake too late, Rosie turned to grab a pillow to fluff as a defense mechanism, but Declan was too quick for her. His large hand closed gently around her wrist, preventing her from exercising the diversionary tactic.

"Rosie." She inhaled slowly and then turned her face away from him as she sat back down. "You even what?"

"I used hearth magic!" she confessed a touch more loudly than she had intended, and then followed up with a hushed explanation. "Or I thought I did, anyway. I found this ritual online involving salt and making a charm bag."

Declan was staring at her, an unasked question lingering in his eyes. But there was something else there, too. Pride? Rosie deliberately looked away from him. His hand was so warm around her wrist, his skin against hers.

"It didn't work," she said to shoo the look of pride away.

"The hell it didn't," he laughed. "Why'd they come to my caravan instead've ya house, then?" He grinned and shook his head. "Probably didn't make it past the mailbox." Then he peered at her, and his grin morphed into a lop-sided smirk.

"Rosie... you need to be naked for a protection spell."

Heat flooded her face, and she opened her mouth to say something but came up blank. He chuckled at her reaction, his hand still around her arm. He let his finger-tips brush against the inside of her wrist as he let her go. Rosie felt herself shiver, but it wasn't because she was cold.

She looked after his retreating hand, back to his face. "When I was doing the spell, I didn't believe that it would work."

"That'll be why you broke ya window, then." He thumbed over his shoulder and looked at the shards of glass she had swept into a corner. "You have to have intention for these things to work, love."

"But I shocked Terry Holt and didn't even mean to," she said, eyes seeking his for guidance. It was too surreal, and now that she had seen actual magic being performed, she couldn't brush it off the way she had with Terry.

"That was a heat of the moment thing," he explained. "Natural talent, if you will. That all came from within you." He smirked. "You probably felt right shagged after."

She rolled her eyes. "Does everything have to relate back to sex with you?"

"Doesn't have to," he shrugged, his eyes twinkling. "It's just more fun that way." He gestured. "In all seriousness, though, that's the difference. Charms and the like—hexes, curses, etcetera—they rely on the three I's: intent, ingredients, incantation."

Rosie gawked at him. "You're not seriously telling me that there's theory behind my allegedly being a witch, are you?"

Declan huffed and rubbed his fingers over his eyes and across the bridge of his nose. "There's no allegedly to it. You're important, Rosie. Not just to Maggie and me, but to the world. We need to make sure that you're up to speed on what that means."

She laughed. She couldn't help it. She wasn't sure if it was because the thought of her being a witch queen was ludicrous, or because she was starting to believe that she might be one after all. "What exactly are you proposing? Witchery 101?"

Declan shrugged a shoulder. "Works for me. And 102 and 103. If your ex is willin' to set fire to things, you're gonna need as much as I can teach ya."

Rosie felt stunned all over again. She couldn't believe that Randy would stoop so low as trying to murder someone. But if he was capable of attempted murder, what did it mean for when he eventually caught up with her?

Because now Rosie was convinced that he would catch up with her. The shadow surrounding her ex-husband got darker with each day. It pressed in on any light she tried to create in her life, and the gathering storm was unavoidable.

She was determined to stay and fight, and if Randy wasn't going to fight fair, maybe she shouldn't, either.

"Alright," she said.

Declan blinked at her. "You mean it?"

She took a deep breath, gripping the edge of the couch. "Yeah. Let's do it."

He let his gaze drop, looking her over, and then he nodded. "Alright. We'll start tomorrow."

CHAPTER EIGHT

His arms wrapped around her felt so good, pressing her into the bed and cuddling her to his chest. Her hands explored his trim chest and stomach, and she marveled at how chiseled he was under those flannel shirts he wore. When one of his hands grasped her backside, she moaned. He dipped his head so that he could hear her pleasure better, his breath falling in short, desperate bursts against the sensitive skin at her collarbone.

"Heavy lies the head that wears the crown," he murmured against her breast as he nuzzled it, moving further down.

"What?" she asked, sitting upright.

Her room was the same as it had been hours before-hand, lit by the soft glow of a night-light she kept on in case she had to check on Maggie. She looked at the bed to her left and found it empty, breathing a ragged sigh of relief mixed with frustration. She was alone, but the lingering sense of breathlessness and euphoria had her blushing anyway.

When she tapped the screen of her new phone and saw that it was only 5:17 am, Rosie groaned and flopped back onto her pillow. After lying awake for a full twenty minutes, Rosie decided that she could get up and tidy the kitchen. She threw on her robe and tiptoed into the front hall, fighting back a blush as she peeked around the corner of the living room wall to check on Declan. And when she saw the state of him, she wished she hadn't.

He sprawled across the couch, a blanket draped across his hips. The waistband of the jeans he'd slept in peeked out from beneath. His bare chest—which was far more glorious than Rosie had been able to imagine in her wildest sex-dreams—rose and fell softly as he continued to sleep. One arm was above his head, revealing both a deliciously posed bicep and exposed abs. If Rosie's eyes got any bigger, they'd have been protruding like a cartoon character's.

"Mom? What are you doing?"

"Gah!"

Rosie jumped, flailing her arms in the air. The noise was more than enough to wake Declan. He leaped off the couch with a grace that should not have belonged to a man who was sleeping soundly, not five seconds beforehand.

"How many times do I have to tell you not to sneak

up on me!" Rosie put a hand to her chest and glared at Maggie, who furrowed her brow.

"I wasn't sneaking!" she protested, "It's not my fault you were too busy staring at Declan to hear me!"

Declan's eyebrows shot upwards, his mouth twisting into a grin before Rosie turned her back on him so she could concentrate on Maggie. "I was *not* staring at Declan," she lied, "I was walking out of my room to go and make breakfast for everyone."

"It's too early for breakfast," Maggie said suspiciously.

"It's too early for you to be awake, yet here we are!" Rosie countered.

"Girls, girls," Declan said then, his accent almost enough to make the admonishment sound charming, but not quite. Maggie and Rosie both rounded on him, and he held his hands up in surrender. "Breakfast sounds grand," he concluded wisely.

"THE PERFECT PANCAKE'S AN ART FORM," DECLAN TOLD Maggie as the pair of them stood over the stove in the kitchen. Maggie was clutching a spatula, and Declan was carefully pouring pancake batter into a griddle at her command.

"No way," Maggie fired back, her face full of skepticism. "Anyone can cook a pancake."

Rosie looked up from the news she was reading on

her phone, her hand curled around the cup of hot coffee Declan had made her. She watched the pair of them interacting, sharing time. It made her sad and angry all at once. It had been years since Randy had shown that kind of interest in anything Maggie did.

"Do you really think it's easy?" she asked Maggie, glancing at him before looking back to her daughter for an answer.

"She'll find out," said Declan. Maggie grinned, shrugged, and then started poking the pancakes with her spatula.

"They're not ready yet," Declan warned her, but he was too late.

"I love pancake mush," Rosie announced.

Declan met her gaze. "Me too."

Rosie blushed and went to go back to her phone, but Maggie had other ideas.

"Mom, I'm not good at flipping pancakes yet." Oh, the irony of five seconds passed. "Can you help Declan?" She waved the spatula. "Please? He said he couldn't do it without supervision."

Rosie knew that had been his way of getting Maggie to help—but it had come back to bite Rosie in the butt. She couldn't very well say no when he needed supervision, could she? Declan paused in scraping the pancake mush out of the skillet long enough to raise a brow at her inquiringly.

"Sure," she murmured, hopping off her stool and making her way over to assume spatula duty. "But if

I'm making breakfast, you need to make your bed. Okay?"

"Okay!"

The kitchen was quiet except for the muted sizzling of pancakes. Rosie and Declan stood at the stove, their arms brushing as they waited for the freshly poured batter to start to bubble.

"You know, breakfast in bed would have been a better option than this," he murmured cheekily. That was all it took for her blush to come back with a vengeance. She could feel the warmth of his breath on the side of her neck, and she resisted the urge to shiver even as she felt a tingle below her belly. His accent was so damned sexy.

Rosie bit the inside of her cheek and took a teensy step away from him, hoping he wouldn't notice.

"You don't even have a bed right now," she said loftily. "So, don't push your luck."

"I wasn't talking about having breakfast in my bed," he grinned, leaning towards her to close the gap she'd created. His face was mere inches from hers, and she had to make an impossible decision between looking into his eyes or looking at his lips as they closed in on her. She gave in and glanced at his mouth, expecting it to reach hers any second, when she felt the spatula slide out of her grip. He retreated with a roguish grin, spatula in hand.

It took her a moment to realize what he'd done. When she cottoned on to the fact that his teasing had been a diversionary tactic, Rosie narrowed her eyes at him.

"First of all," she said, annoyed, "you will never have breakfast in my bed. Ever." He chuckled, which only served to irritate her even more. "Secondly, you need to keep out of my personal space. I have a child in this house, and I won't have her seeing you behave in a lewd way towards her mother!"

At the last bit, Declan seemed to sober up some. "You're right, darlin'. I'm sorry."

She was so shocked by his immediately agreeing with her that she was almost sorry she had been so forceful. But she couldn't very well take it back now, and she had meant it. Just not forever. She huffed out a breath.

"I should think so," she said pertly. She plucked the spatula out of his hand and running it underneath the closest pancake. She flipped it, and it landed perfectly cooked side up.

"YOU NEED TO FOCUS YOUR INTENT," DECLAN INSISTED as they stood side by side on the living room carpet. His hands were on his hips in the pose any good coach adopted when giving a pep talk at the bottom of the ninth. "Make sure ya thinkin' clearly, and with determination."

"I have never been more determined to not have

broken glass all over my living room, or to avoid paying for a repairman to come out and fix it for me," Rosie muttered sarcastically. Declan quirked a brow at her.

"Oh, aye," he said with a disbelieving shake of his head, "You can make as much fun as ya like now. But at 3 am when the wind's howling through your house, and you can't sleep worth a wink, you'll be sorry you didn't pay more attention!"

"I have every confidence that you'll fix it for me before it gets to that," Rosie replied with a sassy grin, "seeing as you'll be the one on the couch sweatin' your —what is it y'all call them? Bollocks? Yeah. Sweatin' your *bollocks* off."

Declan smirked because he knew full well that she was right.

"I never thought I would ever say this," he admitted, his eyes suddenly filled with a look that was somehow sexy and infuriating all at once. "But, you need to stop worrying about my bollocks and focus on the window."

She sighed. The truth was, she wasn't convinced she could even do this, and she was avoiding starting so she wouldn't find out how powerless she was to stop Randy after all. She swallowed as she looked through the broken window at the shards of glass and shook her head. She took a deep breath.

"Say it again," she said.

He lowered his voice. She wouldn't have pegged him as the patient sort. But while he was explaining the process of mending with magic for what must have been the fourth time, he showed no frustration.

"Focus on the window. You're restoring what once was. The glass shards are new things, they used to be the window, but they're somethin' different now. We want them to go back to bein' the window."

He placed a hand on her shoulder, briefly interrupting her concentration, but then his soothing voice brought her focus back onto what she was doing. "Focus on the window."

She took a deep breath and closed her eyes, steadying herself and centering in the moment. She pushed out with her mind, and her external consciousness hit the wall of the cottage. It began to send out fingers, gliding along the wood-paneling, feeling out the area. Rosie's attention flickered for a moment, but then she strengthened her resolve.

"Feel the wall?" Declan asked quietly.

"Yes," she huffed, trying to contain her intent while maintaining contact with the wall itself.

"Great. Now feel it for the window frame."

Easier said than done, Rosie thought, as she began to run her 'hands' over the surface of the wall. When her senses felt the texture of the wall change from wood to unfinished glass, she stopped.

"Good," Declan encouraged her. "Now hone your intent on the unbroken window, the way it was before."

Rosie felt downright silly. This was an imagination game. So, anything she imagined would just happen?

She didn't want that power. What if she imagined something horrible?

"You're not focused," Declan chided.

She sighed. "This feels dumb," she said, realizing even as she said it that it sounded like something Maggie would say. "Can I just pretend it's fixed?"

"You don't have to pretend anythin'," he corrected gently. "You remember the window. You spent all that time cleaning up the drapes around it, didn't ya? You must have loved it a little to do all that work to make it look nice."

He moved to stand behind her, a hand on either shoulder, as though to aim her at the problem. His voice reverberated down the back of her neck as he coached her, and it did help her focus.

"Repairin' things is all about findin' a little love for it," he told her. "For the way it used to be when it was whole, before it was broken. Try again."

She did. This time, when she got to the large cut of glass, she felt a pang of heartbreak at the broken window. When she had first arrived at Fox Cottage, she had sat at that window and looked out the antique panes of glass into the front yard, where the old oak tree stood. How many moons had that window seen? How many conversations had it heard? She remembered being so grateful to the cottage for taking her and Maggie in that she would do anything to protect and brighten it. She felt her determination grow as she thought about how strong and beautiful the glass in the window had once been.

"Open your eyes," Declan's voice interrupted, his hands disappearing from her shoulders.

She released the last of the breath she'd been holding in one big explosion of relief. She was afraid to, lest she find she hadn't done anything at all, but when she opened her eyes, her jaw dropped.

The window was repaired, and more than that, it was clear and clean, as it probably hadn't been since it was built some hundred years ago. The swirls in the glass that she had so admired were still there, but even thicker than before, stronger. The sunlight cast beautiful refracted circles of light on the floor and walls, twinkling in celebration of her accomplishment.

"It's beautiful," she said in wonder.

Declan nodded. "Nice work," he told her with a playful grin as he stepped in front of her. "We'll work on some breathing exercises next. Can't have you passing out mid-cast, no matter how adorable you look when you're concentratin'."

She pinned him with a mock glare. "Well, I mean, I'm a baby witch, so I guess it will take time to work this all out. But thanks for teasin'!"

His grin disappeared. "Rosie, you need to understand how powerful you are. By the time we've unlocked ya true magical ability...." he trailed off, shaking his head as though awed. "You're gonna be one of the most powerful witches on the planet."

Rosie looked at him for a moment, her grey eyes wide with the implication of being a magical superstar. And she burst into laughter.

"So not only am I a Queen—"

"Witch Queen," he corrected her.

"—Witch Queen," she continued, "but I am also one of the most powerful witches in the entire world? These are actual words coming out of your mouth right now?"

The modernism was entirely lost on him. "You come from one of the most ancient magical bloodlines there are," he said. "I'm not makin' this up. You were given up by your parents because they were afraid of your ability."

Rosie felt a chill, thinking back to that day on the dock when she had told him about being in foster care. "Wait—what? How do you know about—"

"Turns out they were right to be worried," he added. "They were killed shortly afterwards. But luckily, the people who killed them never found you."

"The homes I moved around to," Rosie said carefully, not wanting to get emotional, "were hell on earth, and I would hardly call my experience lucky. And how do you know why my parents gave me up?"

He looked at her for what seemed like an age. "Because you and I were promised to each other a very, very long time ago."

"What, like some kind of arranged marriage?" she spluttered, unable to believe what she was hearing.

"Exactly like that," he said to her. She studied his

expression for signs that he was joking but came up empty-handed.

"I'm not marrying someone I'm not in love with!" she exclaimed, fire in her belly. "—again," she added before he could do it for her. "Besides, I don't even know anything about you—or myself, apparently!"

He narrowed his eyes as he looked at her. She could feel her cheeks flushing as she thought back to her dream that morning. He took a deep breath and closed his eyes, slipping his hand into the pocket of his jeans. When he drew it out again, he was holding something tiny. Something round that glinted in the light coming through her gorgeous new window.

A ring. *It was a ring.*

Holy shitballs, he was going to propose.

She watched him, horrified, until he bowed his head in respect to her.

"I am *Áed*. Son of *Áine*, protector of *coróin an tsamhraidh*." He glanced up at her, looking for all the world like an ancient Celtic king throwing himself at the mercy of a fair maiden. She almost got carried away by the moment, before she realized that the fair maiden was supposed to be her. She only just managed to stop herself laughing in time for him to take her hand in his.

"You don't have to marry me in a conventional sense," he told her. "It's not like we have a magical marriage registry office. But our binding will unite the people of my world and the people of yours. It will provide strength, protection, and prosperity on both sides of the union."

"My people?" Rosie did laugh, then. "I don't even know who my people are! I'm not even sure I want to if they're content to let their alleged Queen go from foster home to foster home, and then wind up with a guy who treated her like shit for decades! And I don't have to marry you at all—just so we're clear on that," she added for good measure.

Declan smiled up at her wistfully. "You're the Queen of the Lost," he said, "All the ones who don't have kingdoms or families to look after 'em. And you have suffered," he agreed with her, "but not at the hands or even the knowledge of your people. They don't know you exist yet. They just know you're out there somewhere."

Then he held up the ring for her to see. It was a plain simple band of hammered copper that parted in the middle. "This is a promise," he told her. "Of my protection, faithfulness, and fealty to you as your betrothed King and consort."

She frowned, already seeing a problem. "It's broken," she announced. "What kind of promise is made with a ring that doesn't go all the way 'round?"

"It's not broken," he chuckled. "The promise starts now, he pointed to one side of the ring, "and is complete when we're joined." He pointed to the other side of the ring.

She quirked a brow, not buying it. "What happens to the promise then?"

He shook his head with a smile. "New ring, new promise. Will you accept it?"

Protection. Faithfulness. Fealty. Who couldn't use a little – or a lot?—of those things? But Rosie had gone down this track before. She'd come to learn that wearing a guy's ring might as well mean that you're his property. And then an idea came to her.

"I'll make you a counter-offer," she told him. She took him by his free hand and tugging him up until he stood towering over her once more.

He looked down at her, curiosity burning in his gaze. "Let's hear it."

She licked her lips and looked down to stare at the ring he still clasped. "I'll wear this ring as a symbol of our growing friendship. And in return for your protection, faithfulness, and fealty as my friend," she then lifted her eyes to meet his. "I offer you those same things in friendship myself."

He studied her for a long moment. The corners of his eyes crinkled in a way that told her he might very well laugh in her face. But the mirth spread across his face, and soon she was basking in the glow of his warm, boyish grin.

"Deal," he said, and he reached for her hand, slipping the ring onto the fourth finger of her right hand. The same tingles that had prickled her skin when he had passed her the cherry from Maggie's ice cream sundae ran out of the ring and through her skin, coursing through veins in her arm.

"Whoa," she breathed, taking her arm back and holding it up to look at it in wonder. "What was that?"

"A protection spell," he told her. "You're a way off being able to conjure one of them yourself yet, so this one will do until then."

Relief washed over her, feeling like the healing waters of her bath the other night. A protection spell from someone who could do magic, instead of her half-working hearth magic, was a stellar improvement.

"Thanks," Rosie said gratefully. She held her ring up to look at it in the late afternoon sunlight streaming through the window. And then a thought occurred to her.

"Do you think you could do something similar for Maggie?"

Declan didn't even skip a beat. "Of course."

Rosie offered him a broad smile, her relief beginning to pick at undoing the anxious knot in her stomach. "Thank you," she said, then looked around at her better-than-before living room. "So... what happens next?"

"When we're ready, you'll have a coronation so that your people can revel in your presence and chant your name. "We don't have to consummate our binding until you're ready," he added, a roguish smile tugging at his lips."

It took a moment for the implication of his words to

sink in. She thwacked him on the shoulder with the back of her hand.

"I was talking about dinner!" she cried. "Lord. Just because you helped me fix the window doesn't mean you won't still be sleeping in the swamp if the Queen commands it," she warned him.

He laughed. She turned to leave, but he caught her by the hand and looked into her eyes.

"Well done, Rosie," he said to her. He glanced at the window and then looked back to her, a tired smile on his face.

"You did most of it," she said self-deprecatingly. "I don't even know the basics of magic. I'll—"

"Learn," he said. Before she knew what he was doing, he had folded her into an enormous, warm hug.

Her first instinct was to stiffen. She couldn't remember Randy ever hugging her—and she didn't want to remember if he had. She resisted the temptation to tense up and instead let his body heat envelop her. Her hands rested on his brown leather belt on either side of his hips. His clean, wholesome aroma of cedar mixed with what she could only describe as a combination of sweet whiskey and butterscotch cookies surrounded her. It was delicious, and that was before he bent his head to press a quick, boundary-pushing kiss to the top of her long dark locks.

"C'mon," he murmured into her hair.

"What?" she asked. C'mon what? Her heart was beating faster than it had in decades from just a hug and a head-kiss. If he made a move on her, she was sure that her lady-parts would explode into flames.

"You were asking about dinner," he reminded her, his voice tinged with amusement that told her he had guessed her thoughts.

"Oh!" she said, straightening and stepping away from him. "Of course."

She paused before leaving the room to look at the now glittering window in the front room. She shook her head.

Great. Now she'd have to wash the other windows to match.

CHAPTER NINE

"You're sure she's asleep?" Rosie tried to peer past Declan to get a view of Maggie in her bed down the hall.

"Yes," he declared, looking rather pleased with himself. "Out like a light. So, don't be wakin' her, mumma-bear. Let the cub sleep."

Rosie smiled, ignoring the bone-tiredness that seeped in as soon as she stepped out of her shower.

True to his word, Declan had rustled up a simple dinner in the kitchen and laid it on the counter. She pulled up a stool as he served them both generous helpings of leftover mashed potatoes and gravy with a side of beans. She watched him set out their cutlery, his large hand surprisingly deft at sprinkling just the right amount of salt and pepper over their feast.

"Smells great," Rosie said, smiling up at him as he rounded the counter to park himself beside her.

"Good," he replied with a satisfied nod. "You need to eat. If you don't clean ya bowl, there'll be no dessert."

"Dessert?" Rosie's ears pricked up. What she wouldn't give for a piece of angel cake. Or some plain, creamy chocolate. And then she deflated. "I don't have anything sweet in the house," she sighed.

"That's not true," Declan told her, scooping up a spoonful of mash. He blew on it for a second, and Rosie watched the soft pout his lips made until he spoke again. "You're about the sweetest person I ever met," he said, shoveling in his mash-and-beans.

The compliment caught her off guard. She felt a tiny flutter of something light and pleasant in her stomach. And then she realized that he had meant he'd like her for dessert. A blush bloomed across her cheeks in time for him to nod at her.

"Exceptin' Maggie, a-course," around a mouth full of mashed potato.

Rosie laughed, tucking into her dinner. It was such a simple, wholesome compliment that it came quite unexpectedly from Declan, who didn't seem able to take anything seriously. But more than that, it was totally the opposite of Randy's compliments. Randy only ever said things about how she looked or what she wore, or what sexual thing he'd been planning in his head.

They ate quietly, the sounds of the cottage creaking and the trees swaying in the stiff summer breeze outside keeping real silence at bay. By the time they had both emptied their bowls, Rosie felt like she could have crawled into bed for a week.

She was tempted. The trials of being a single mom mandated that you are on the clock 24/7. There were no sick days, or overtime, or substitutes you could call in. And, she thought as she hopped up and collected the bowls and cutlery to place in the sink, she had been a single mom ever since Maggie had been born.

Randy hadn't ever been interested in the nuances of raising babies, and she had been only too happy to be Maggie's world. But the last few days had started to open her eyes about how it could have been. What it would have been like for Maggie to have a dad to play on the lawn with. How it would have felt to make a big family breakfast together on Sunday mornings.

What it would have been like to have someone in her life who had wanted her, too.

She turned away from stacking the sink and almost ran straight into Declan.

"Oh!" she uttered before a breathy laugh escaped her. "Sorry!"

He smiled down at her but didn't move to get out of the way so that she could pass him. Rosie met his gaze, her embarrassment at nearly colliding with him morphed into confusion.

"I'm heading to bed," she announced in a hushed version of her too-chipper voice. Her earlier blush had returned in full force, and she was starting to think he meant to kiss her in the kitchen. She didn't know how she would feel about that – which told her that she wasn't ready to feel anything about it at all.

"Goodnight!" She flashed him a strained smile and made to step around him, but he reached out and took her hand.

"There's one more thing we need to do," he told her. His voice was soft and husky, and the heat of his palm against hers made that fluttering feeling from her stomach explode.

"I'm beat," she said with a little more force. "I need to go to bed, Declan."

"If we don't re-do the wards, then we're left exposed," he said pointedly, letting go of her hand.

She mentally stepped back from where she thought this had been going. Her brain slipped out of the half-panic, half-tempted fog it had bogged down in. "The wards?"

"Yes. The moon is perfect, and there are two of us this time." His expression was earnest, but the spark of cheek in his eyes reminded her of an important detail.

"But... hearth magic has to be cast while naked," she reminded herself.

He dipped his head to one side, his lips pulled in a half-smile. "I won't look if you don't," he teased.

Rosie had forgotten about the wards after the excitement of being able to use magic to fix the window and the exhaustion that followed. The thought of stripping down to her birthday suit in front of Declan filled her with dread. She already had a hard time believing that someone like him would even look twice at her. She didn't need to confirm those beliefs by having him gawking at her stretch marks.

But, what if learning to do this properly could help her keep Maggie safe? What if Declan was right and she really was a witch, and her magical powers were starting to build? Was she so ashamed of her naked body, which nature had given her, that she wouldn't use it to protect her child?

She focused on taking a deep breath, letting the air fill her lungs as though she thought it would give her the strength to say what she was about to say. Tilting her chin up in a look that was half defiance, half nerves, and all sass, she nodded.

"Let's do it."

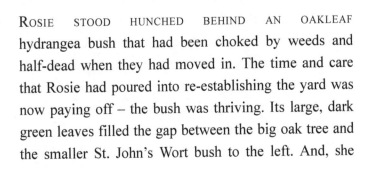

Rosie stood hunched behind an oakleaf hydrangea bush that had been choked by weeds and half-dead when they had moved in. The time and care that Rosie had poured into re-establishing the yard was now paying off – the bush was thriving. Its large, dark green leaves filled the gap between the big oak tree and the smaller St. John's Wort bush to the left. And, she thought to herself as she drank in the soft, honey-scented aroma of the delicate white blooms on the hydrangea, it provided the perfect dressing screen.

Declan was standing not too far away. She heard him pull his shirt over his head, and the rustle of leaves as he hung it on a branch. The tell-tale *zwip!* of his zipper being undone came next.

Rosie shimmied out of her denim shorts and felt the heat in the breeze coast over her lower body. She glanced down, ignoring the fact that she desperately needed some new underwear. True to Declan's word, the moon shone thick, milky light over the whole clearing, including on the cellulite dimples she could see high-lighted on her upper thighs. Rosie tugged her tank top over her head, making sure her ponytail was still in place. Then she unclipped her bra.

Gravity was a cruel mistress. Without the support of the underwire, her breasts didn't have the same shape they'd had at seventeen. Her stomach was a tight knot of nerves. She bent down, hooking her thumbs into the waistband of her panties. She pushed them down her legs quickly as though she was removing a Band-Aid. As soon as her body was free from fabric, Rosie broke out in goosebumps despite the warm summer night.

It was as though the moon itself was greeting her skin. A sense of recognition filtered through the air to settle on her shoulders like a gossamer mantle. On instinct, Rosie reached up to her ponytail and pulled at the hairband, releasing her long dark curls. They fell over her shoulders, hugging her breasts and hanging down the middle of her back. She hoped that the added coverage would help conceal a little of her boob-sag, but the overall feeling was incredibly sensual, which was rather inconvenient because she didn't want to feel sensual.

She wanted to feel like a badass witch.

"Rosie?" Declan's voice drifted across the garden to her, and she felt her breath catch in the back of her throat. She snatched a branch of the bush, pulling it against her skin like a shield.

"What?" she called back in an exaggerated whisper.

"Ready?"

Taking a deep breath that she immediately let out again once she noticed it made it look like her bosom was heaving, Rosie steeled herself. "I guess," she muttered.

When he spoke again, Declan sounded much closer than before. "What?"

"I said yes!" she yelped, moving closer to the bush as she tried to see where he was standing. She could almost make him out, standing on the lawn a few yards away.

He paused, and it seemed like he wanted to say something but then thought better of it. "Okay, you go around the house in a clockwise direction – I'll go anti-clockwise. Like you did the first time, only this time with more intent. Between the two of us, we should be able to double-charge the wards."

In her head, Rosie was already planning the route she would take to get maximum coverage. She wasn't sure whether success in this instance would having wards strong enough to keep Randy and his men at bay or by being able to run around the house completely nude without Declan seeing her. At last, she replied with a terse, "Okay," and bent down to retrieve the carton of rock-salt by her abandoned flip-flops.

"Great. Let's go."

He didn't need to tell her twice. Rosie turned her back on him and adopted a weird lope that was equal parts skipping and running, trying not to knock herself out with her jiggling boobs. She gave up three paces into her crossing of the lawn. Scooping her breasts up with one arm across her chest, she clutched her carton of salt with the other. She sprinkled as she galloped but forgot that she was also supposed to be chanting until she reached the relative comfort of the oak tree garden bed in the middle of the lawn.

"Shit," she huffed, trying to catch her breath from her first effort. She turned to face the trunk of the tree, standing close enough so that it would cover the front of her body from view. Sprinkling salt around the base clockwise, Rosie reached around the trunk, almost like she was hugging the tree, and passed the salt carton to herself.

"Mother Moon, please hear my call," she began,

straining to remember the chant. "Uhh... I don't remember the rest at all!"

Her admission forced an unexpected giggle out of her, which she stifled by clapping her hand over her mouth. When she was sure that she wouldn't laugh again, she decided that honesty would be the best policy and that it was time for some real talk.

"Look, Mother Moon," she said, feeling ridiculous. "I don't remember this chant, and it seems kind of dumb to say it anyway. You know my intentions – they're in my heart." Rosie pursed her lips. "I need to protect my kid from her father, and I'm willing to do whatever it takes to do it. Ain't no intention purer than a mother's love."

She looked straight up into the full, clear moon, bright and white on the summer evening. "So please hear me. I need your help."

She stood there for a long moment, her arms around the oak tree and her body pressed to the bark. The breeze swayed the air around her, and it felt like a mother's soothing caress. Rosie took it to mean that she had the Moon's blessing, and she smiled. "Thank you," she whispered.

Rosie peeked around the tree trunk. Seeing no sign of Declan, she decided to dash her next location – the corner of the cottage. She gripped her salt carton, supported her boobs once more, and took off. A thin trickle of salt drifted to the ground in her wake as she made the sprint in record time. She paused in the darkness beside the cottage. After a quick pause to catch her breath, she began to walk the length of the wall, trailing salt as she went. Just a little further, and she'd be on the home stretch.

She rounded the corner at a walk, and then stopped in her tracks. Declan was directly across from her, weaving his way through a copse of baby pine trees. He hadn't seen her and continued to mumble the incantation under his breath as he worked. Rosie almost panicked and dashed back behind the wall of the house, but it was as though the calming influence of the moonlight made her relax.

So instead of making a run back behind the wall to safety, she moved forwards. Her eyes coasted over Declan, from the serious expression on his face that she caught as he moved between patches of moonlight and shadow, down over the broad strength of his shoulders. But she didn't stop there. Rosie came to stand behind a straggly dogwood hedge. She took in the taut muscles of his belly, the purposeful movement of his thighs.

She drank in the rest of him with pleasure, watching him turn back toward the house. It wasn't until she looked back up to his face that she noticed him staring at her. Instead of snatching branches of the hedge to cover herself better, she stood tall. His gaze fell, following the dark cascade of her hair to her breasts and then back up. When their eyes met again, his were stormy, the green of a northern sea lashing a dark, rugged coast.

"Are ya finished?" he asked her, his voice husky.

She could hear the blatant desire in his tone. Her body responded by breaking out into goosebumps all over again. She didn't know whether he was referring to the hearth magic or her staring at him, and she considered the question before giving her answer.

"Yes," she said, her eyes skipping between his.

He studied her face and then nodded gruffly as though trying to shake himself out of a dream. "I'll... uh." He cleared his throat.

The sound made her realize the effect she was having on him. He tried not to let his eyes fall to look at her nakedness. But even though he failed on several occasions, Rosie knew that he wasn't looking to find fault with her. He wasn't looking with a critical eye. He was looking with restrained hunger, with desire.

And that knowledge made her feel like a badass witch after all.

"I'll turn around so you can get your clothes on," he told her and promptly turned his back.

The Rosie of five minutes ago would have been grateful for the opportunity and made the most of it. But now Rosie could feel something powerful building inside of her. It was fierce strength, smoldering in her belly in a way that told her it would soon burst into fire. The hint of a wicked smile tugged at her lips as she made her way around the end of the hedge, walking straight up to Declan.

She reached for his hand, entwining their fingers. He

turned to look over his shoulder at her in surprise, and when he noticed her expression, a look of recognition overcame him. His answering grin was bold and celebratory, and it encouraged the first flickers of her confidence to unfurl. They walked together, hand in hand, to collect their clothes and get dressed.

CHAPTER TEN

For a while, Rosie's life settled down into a groove that was close to normal as she'd ever known. Maggie had summer reading, and she had work. They went for a quick walk through different parts of town on their way home each afternoon, starting to get to know their surroundings. She didn't have friends, and women her age in town now seemed to avoid the Go-Go-Mart like the plague. Rosie felt that she was okay with a quieter existence.

Maggie had insisted on spending the afternoon with Declan. They were headed to Wood & Wax to get supplies for the deck repairs he was doing. Rosie wandered into the Kwik Kleen. It was fast becoming her least favorite place to be despite her initial excitement. The small, dingy room looked like it hadn't seen a lick of paint or a spit of disinfectant in years, which probably accounted for the musty smell.

Washers and dryers were crammed against one another along the back wall. An uncomfortable outdoor bench hunched by the door, scattered with outdated magazines. The noticeboard where Rosie found her job perched above the seat, threatening to fall on anyone who dared sit beneath it.

The only good thing about the place was the full-length windows that made up the entire storefront and let in plenty of sunshine. She moved to the machine closest to the door and began to stuff her dirty laundry inside. She added a detergent pod and eyed the machine warily. She was in no mood for linoleum gymnastics today.

"Listen up," she said to it, meaning business. "I don't want any funny business today. I need this done in time for my shift. Got it?"

The machine just sat there.

Rosie dug out her purse and put three quarters down the coin slot. They dropped into the machine with a ka-chink, ka-chink, ka-chink. Pressing her lips together and crossing her fingers on both hands, she reached forward with one middle finger to press the 'wash' button.

Nothing happened. Rosie could feel the rage starting to build in her, that sense of resentment that of course the damn washing machine would continue to eat her change, because she didn't have an infinite supply of cash and couldn't afford her own damn washing machine.

She squared her shoulders and glared at the

offending appliance, determined that she would get her laundry done come hell or high water.

"I've broken stuff before, you know," she warned the machine. "I have a fried cell phone to prove it."

The machine didn't seem bothered.

"Ugh!" Frowning, Rosie decided that she needed to take serious action. Now was as good a time as any to test her so-called magical powers, right? No one was around. No one would be able to report on her actions for the Mosswood Messenger. With a deep breath, she faced the machine and laid her hands on the display panel.

As she let her breath out, she focused her entire body on transferring energy to the washing machine. She tried to remember what Declan had said about The Three I's, but as she didn't have any ingredients, she would have to make do with the other two. Intent? Check. That left...

"Wash my damn clothes, you temperamental sono-fabitch," Rosie intoned as mystically as possible.

She gave the machine a final push of energy. She could feel it hum as it left her hands, vibrating against the plastic dial and display panel of the machine before it dissipated. And nothing happened at all.

Rosie saw red. "You piece of—!" She lashed out and landed a kick on the bottom of the machine.

Whirr.

The machine grumbled to action just as Rosie was prepping to lose her shit. She held her breath for a couple of seconds, daring it to stop after teasing her with potential competence. When it continued into the wash cycle, she exhaled and stepped away so as not to disturb it.

"Typical," she muttered, making her way over to the messy bench to wait out her sentence.

WHEN ROSIE'S CELL BEEPED TOWARDS THE END OF HER shift, she knew it could only be one person. She smiled, a little flutter of something that felt like excitement tickled her stomach before she shooed it away. Excitement wasn't something she needed to be associating with anyone right now, much less her newly acquired and often irritating house guest.

Sure enough, a notification from Declan sat at the top of her screen. Her day had been peppered with texts and pictures of what he and Maggie were up to: enjoying hot dogs at Granny's for lunch, laying out tools when they got home, Maggie looking pleased as punch to be strong enough to carry one of the decking boards from the truck to the house all by herself. It was adorable, and Rosie had been devouring the updates. She unlocked her phone to read the text.

'Would you like us to pick you up from work?'

Warmth bloomed in the pit of her stomach, and her

smile widened. That was kind of him. She was tempted to say yes on account of the heat, but she liked her walks. They gave her time to think about what might be next for her while also letting her soak in her new surroundings and get a little exercise. And today, even though she still had to carry laundry, she had the bonus of having the walk to herself because Maggie was already with Declan.

'No thanks – I'm all set. See you guys soon.'

She finished out the last ten minutes of her shift, tidying up the counter area and restocking the gum stand one last time. After offering Ben a cheerful goodbye that he returned from the far end of aisle two, Rosie set out up Main Street. The sun had already sunk to the forest canopy, and she hadn't even made it past the Elementary School before it slipped behind the trees.

There was still plenty of light, but now it was the golden, buttery kind that drenched everything in high-lights of gold and shadows of blue-green. It was this time of day in the summer that Rosie liked best; the cicadas would start up, the frogs croaked from down by the river. She didn't feel any hesitation as she walked out of town and up the long, winding road towards what Ben had told her was Needlepoint Woods. As she approached the cottage through a thick part of the woods, she could hear shrieks.

Maggie.

Rosie's heart leaped into her throat, and she abandoned the road to run through the woods towards the sound in a blind panic. It was still light enough to see when she burst through the trees beside the lawn, and she stopped dead in her tracks as another shriek filled the air, followed immediately by a cascade of giggles.

Maggie and Declan were chasing each other across the lawn, skittering in circular motions with arms stretched wide, trying to tag each other back. They were both drenched from head to foot by the spray of a lone sprinkler that Declan must have picked up from the Wood & Wax. Maggie's hair was plastered to her head, and she wore a smile so wide that Rosie began to tear up.

And then she noticed what Declan was wearing. A pair of cargo shorts and that was it. His muscles bunched and shifted with effort as he ran, and Rosie found herself mesmerized by the droplets of water that were speckled over his pale skin, catching the last rays of sunlight. He shook his head as he ran after Maggie, water spraying in all directions, and his ginger hair spiking up in every which way. He roared with laughter as he tagged Maggie back and turned to evade her, spotting Rosie standing across the lawn.

"There ya are!" he called with a grin, slowing down to catch his breath enough to talk. "We were worried you were gonna miss out on all the fun!"

"Come on, Mom!" Maggie chimed in, dancing

across the lawn like a wood sprite to catch hold of her mother's hand. "You and me can gang up on Declan!"

"Oh aye, that sounds about right," he complained, bending at the waist to rest the heels of his palms on his knees. "Two against one – I see how it is!"

Her panic eased, Rosie shrugged a shoulder. "I dunno," she said. She set the bag of laundry down on the dry grass as she allowed Maggie to tow her across the lawn towards the sprinkler. "I think your ego counts as at least one other person – possibly two."

Declan pressed a hand to his heart as though he had been shot. Rosie smirked, rolling her eyes at him. She looked down at her denim shorts and the blue cotton polo shirt with the Go-Go-Mart logo on the breast pocket that formed her uniform. As she shuffled to kick off her plain white tennis shoes, she looked between Declan and Maggie.

"Who's it?"

"You are!" Maggie declared gleefully, leaping forward, and landing a well-placed tap on Rosie's butt.

"Why, you little –!" Rosie laughed, taking off after her daughter through the refreshing spray of the sprinkler as Maggie cackled. The chase continued for several laps of the big oak in the middle of the lawn. Rosie followed Maggie until she could see her daughter was starting to tire. As soon as she was close enough, she feinted to the left before ducking to the right. She paused, tapping an unsuspecting Declan on his beefy shoulder.

"Misdirection is it!" he cried, bolting after Rosie, and earning himself a shriek from her for his effort. By this stage, it was getting dark, and it was much harder to see. Rosie weaved across the lawn, hoping to outrun him, but her walks to and from town weren't effective enough training for this kind of a workout. She felt his hand close over her arm, and she scrambled in one last attempt to get away from him, but her foot slipped in the wet grass.

Before she knew what had happened, she had slipped onto her side. Declan's grip had been so tight on her arm that she had taken him down with her. He landed on the grass beside her with a massive 'oof!', their arms and legs tangled. She took a second to understand what had happened, and still another to know for sure that she wasn't hurting anywhere.

"Are you okay?" she said, listening to Maggie still running and shrieking on the opposite side of the lawn. She was suddenly hyper-aware of their bare, wet skin pressed together, the smell of the grass, the sensation of the water droplets falling from the air. She could barely make out his face in the darkness now, but she knew it was awfully close to hers. She could feel his breath, hot and fast, on her cheek.

"Fine," he said between breaths, his voice husky. "You?"

"I'm fine. I–"

"Dogpile!" Maggie screeched, coming out of nowhere to make a flying leap. She landed on top of the pair of them, making them both groan with pain and indignity.

"Maggie! What–" Rosie began, but the tickling had already started.

Declan tickled Maggie. Maggie tickled Rosie. Rosie was so ticklish that she was incapable of tickling anyone. The three of them rolled on the wet lawn, torturing each other, their laughter filling the surrounding woods. Rosie's face was hurting from all the fun she was having, and she finally managed to break free from being tickled herself long enough to contemplate tickling Declan when a pair of bright lights blinded her.

Headlights.

"Pizza!" Declan and Maggie cried in unison, abandoning the war front to leap to their feet. Declan offered Rosie his hand, and she shook it, hoping that she didn't have grass stains on her drenched work shirt. As she came to her feet, she noticed Declan's eyes skipping over her face in the light from the car. He reached up, plucking off a sprig of grass that had stuck to her cheek and flicking it away.

"Hungry?" he asked her, his expression unreadable.

"Starving," she replied, determined to keep hers neutral as well.

She turned to look at Maggie, who was already badgering the delivery boy as he retrieved their pizza from the car. When he turned and Rosie saw his face, she bit back a groan.

It was Prissy Bishop's son, the sour-faced blonde kid who had been featured alongside his parents in the *Herald of Hope* newsletter. And he had seen her, Rosie Bell: alleged maneater, rolling around in the dirt soaking wet with a huge Irishman who currently looked like he belonged on the cover of a graphic erotica novel.

Maybe she should start accepting lifts to and from town, in case they decided to stone her to death.

"MOM!" MAGGIE CALLED FROM THE OTHER ROOM AS Rosie danced around the stove in the kitchen. "Can we light the fire tonight? And then we can make s'mores, and tell ghost stories, and—"

"Not tonight," Rosie interjected, and Maggie groaned.

"Why not?"

"Because it's ninety degrees outside."

"If it gets cold?" Maggie counter-offered.

Rosie raised a brow. "We'll see."

Satisfied with that answer, for the time being, Maggie fell quiet. Rolling her eyes and shaking her head, Rosie continued to set out paper plates and napkins at the squashed round table. Maggie and Declan were having so much fun in the kitchen earlier she had kicked them out so she could get down to business. Pizza was supposed to be an easy meal.

She lost herself in the relaxing ritual of setting the

table and emptying the sink of dishes. Now that she'd tidied up, the cottage felt homey and safe, her little woodland sanctuary. She put the salt and pepper shakers on the table, and the oven dinged, alerting that the pizza had been re-warmed.

"Dinner!" she called. After a few moments, two pairs of feet sounded in the front hall before Maggie and Declan emerged. The pair of them had soot smeared all over their faces, and Declan's hair was nearly black with it. Rosie stared at them for a moment, taking in the sight of Maggie's happy, smudged little face, and the sheepish expression on Declan's.

"We decided to see if we could dislodge any of the blockage in the fireplace," he admitted.

"Don't worry!' Maggie chimed in, "It didn't get on the couch! Or the rug! Or the—"

"It's mostly just on us," Declan cut her off, throwing her a look that cautioned her not to volunteer too much information until they knew the depth of the trouble they were in.

Rosie looked from one to the other, and then she burst out laughing. The pair of them looked at her and then at each other. Then they fixed her with pearly white grins that stood out starkly from the black streaks all over their faces, which only made Rosie laugh even harder. They joined in. Once their giggles had wound down to a manageable rate, Rosie wiped the tears from her eyes and decided to take charge.

"Well, we can't eat with y'all looking like that.

Declan—please go wash up in the kitchen sink. Maggie – shower."

"Yes, ma'am," he said, giving her a good-natured salute, which Maggie immediately copied before dissolving into giggles again.

Ten minutes later, Rosie returned to find the pizza steaming on top of the stove while Declan dried himself. He clicked his fingers to stop the spell he had been using to keep the food warm. She glanced from the pizza to him and had just enough time to take in the sight of his roguish grin before Maggie joined them.

"Oh, man, I can't wait to eat! Thanks for the pizza, Declan."

Rosie's face glowed with pride at her well-mannered child. She leaned over to press a kiss to the top of Maggie's freshly shampooed and still damp head.

"You're welcome, Magnolia," Declan said, shaking an insane amount of red pepper flakes onto his pizza. "How about a story while we eat?"

Maggie nodded. "Yes, please!"

"Okay," Declan said with a knowing smile, pulling apart his pizza slices so they could cool.

"Once upon a time, there was a beautiful witch princess. She had hair as dark as ebony and sparkling grey eyes that were the same color as the sky after a rainstorm." His eyes met Rosie's across the table. She felt a blush threatening her cheeks, so she focused on her pizza instead.

"Just like mom!" Maggie exclaimed happily.

"Just like your mum." Declan smiled and continued. "This princess looked like her mother, who looked like her mother, who had been the spitting image of her mother, and so on. The princess was the pride and joy of her parents, and they promised her fair hand in marriage to the witch prince of a neighboring land in the hopes that their lands would be joined, forevermore."

Maggie scoffed. "But boys can't be witches! Boy witches are called wizards."

Declan shook his head. "Nope. Wizards are a different kettle of fish – but we'll talk about them another time." He took a bite of his pizza, chewed it a few times, and then swallowed. "Anyway," he said, "the princess was in love with another man, and couldn't abide the thought of marrying someone she wasn't in love with. Her parents were afraid that she would defy their wishes to marry the prince, so they had a terrible spell placed on her."

"Her own parents did?" Maggie asked in a hushed voice. "That's so mean!" She reached for her pizza, leveling it at her mouth without taking her eyes off Declan.

"Mm-hm. Every day that the princess refused to marry the prince, she would lose a little bit of her magic." Declan took another bite. "In dribs and drabs, her magic would dwindle down until finally it would disappear entirely. The princess was so in love that she chose to sacrifice her magic, and she stole away with her beloved in the dead of night. They made their way across the sea, where she was merely a woman instead of a princess. She had to find work as a lowly servant, scrubbing pots and pans. But they were so happy, and their happiness preserved her magic longer than her parents ever expected."

Although the sadness of the story struck her, Rosie could think of worse lives to live. She would much rather have real, true love than riches and a crown. She eyed Declan suspiciously over the table and began to wonder where the story was heading.

He met her gaze, but his expression gave nothing away. "But her magic still diminished over time. Many years later, their only child grew ill. The princess used up all the rest of her magic to keep the babe alive. Feeling the last of her magic ebbing away, she cast one last spell. She implored the moon not to let her parents' cruelty survive forever. That one day, all the magic taken from her would return to her lineage."

A strange chill came over Rosie then, even though the house was sweltering on account of the old, busted AC unit. She had only just had a heart-to-heart with the moon herself recently. There was something hauntingly familiar about this tale even though she'd never heard it before.

"But she didn't know that her parents had also cast a spell," Declan continued. "Regretting having forced their daughter away from them, they had made a promise to the moon—that when their daughter's magic ran dry, they would sacrifice their magic to strengthen hers."

Maggie gasped, and Rosie was so enthralled with the story now that the sound made her jump.

"What would that mean?" Maggie asked, her eyes like saucers.

"Well," Declan said, looking across the table at Rosie pointedly, in a way that said his next words were for her. "That when their daughter's line eventually had her magic restored, it would be powerful beyond all magic known before. And the promise of marriage between those two families?" He nodded somberly. "It still stands, waiting for the magic to return and for The Lost Lineage to reunite the kingdoms."

Maggie stared at him, chewing her pizza thoughtfully. A few seconds after the story had come to its end, she swallowed. "What happens when the families do unite?"

Declan looked away from Rosie and took the last bite of his pizza. "I've got a story about that one'n all, but it's for another day."

"Yes, it's getting late," Rosie agreed. She wasn't sure how to feel about the story at all as she glanced at the rickety old clock on the kitchen wall. "It's time for bed, Maggie."

"Awww," Maggie pouted. The desire to stay up and entertain their cool new houseguest had a bigger draw than Rosie had imagined. "Do I have to?"

"Yep," Rosie replied without blinking. "How do you

think Declan would feel if you were too tired to help clean the fireplace tomorrow?"

"Probably mad," Maggie conceded.

"We wouldn't want that to happen, now would we?" Declan chimed in, starting to collect up the paper plates.

"Mom, can Declan tuck me in tonight?"

Rosie glanced at Declan, who was trying not to seem so pleased about being chosen for the honor.

"I suppose, on one condition."

"What condition?" she asked.

Rosie thought about the other night when they had done the hearth magic, and how he'd said Maggie had fallen into a deep sleep immediately. She didn't feel too bad about it—what mother hadn't wished for her child to just go to sleep already at some point in their parental career? But she didn't exactly love the idea of her kid being magic-ified to sleep either. She leveled a gaze in his direction.

"He knows."

The briefest flicker of guilt passed over his face. "Deal," he sighed with a slight smile. Maggie whooped with excitement. She kissed her mother goodnight and took off at a skipping-jog for her room. Declan stood from the table and pushed his chair in. He bent slightly towards Rosie as he passed behind her chair.

"Spoilsport," he murmured before following Maggie.

CHAPTER ELEVEN

"I t sparkles in the light. Look!" Maggie held the pendant out in front of her for Rosie to see. They both stopped walking to marvel at the way dandelion puff in the small glass ball glittered.

"It's beautiful," Rosie agreed, as they started walking again. "It was very kind of Declan to think of you."

"Yeah," Maggie agreed. Rosie gave mental thanks again for Declan agreeing to give her child the protection charm. It was a fun new bauble for Maggie to admire, but for her, it was a little more peace of mind.

They walked down The Ridge into town, Maggie with her backpack full of activities and Rosie with a sack full of laundry that she would do after her shift.

"I wonder if you can make a wish with it," Rosie said, reaching out to straighten Maggie's curls.

"I've already tried, but nothing happened." Maggie pulled a face, and Rosie smiled.

Rosie smiled, squinting into the bright morning sun as they trekked. "Guess you'll have to wait and see if it comes true. Sometimes these things take a while."

Rosie found her mind drifting as she thought about the story Declan had shared the night before. Up until recently, she'd thought that he was a little nuts. But more and more things were happening that she couldn't explain. Her phone. The candle. Terry. Was there an ancient promise that still waited to be fulfilled?

The sound of a car approaching from behind pulled her from her thoughts. Out of habit, she reached for Maggie's hand and moved in on the shoulder of the road so that they were out of the car's path. Sidewalks only extended to the civilized part of town.

Rosie didn't notice that the car slowed as it approached because she was listening to Maggie talking about dandelions and wishes. As the car rushed past them, a voice rang out across the road.

"Whore!"

The sound was enough to make both Rosie and Maggie turn to look. Rosie caught an egg to the side of her head, the impact dazing her and causing her to stumble. An egg aimed at Maggie landed right in the middle of her chest, smashing and dribbling ooze all over her favorite t-shirt. A few more eggs fell around them and between them, but no more hit their targets.

The pair stood there in shock as the car drove off,

Rosie staring at the receding license plate. And then fury overtook her.

She concentrated on the rest of the eggs she knew must be in the car and narrowed her eyes. A moment later, the sound of something splattering all over the inside of the car echoed down the street. The vehicle swerved before coming to a slow stop.

Rosie gasped. Egg dripped down the inside windows of the SUV, and she breathed, terrified that something awful had happened to the boys inside. The SUV began to move again, corrected itself back into the lane, and then spun its wheels as it peeled away at a much faster pace than it had been going moments before.

"Mom, what was that?"

When she turned to comfort Maggie, her daughter was staring at her, but she had no idea what to say. She opened her mouth, but all the wishful thinking in the world wouldn't make an explanation come to her.

"Here," Maggie then said and bent over to collect weedy leaves for them both. She handed one to Rosie.

"Are you okay?" She asked. It was such a sweet and selfless gesture that Rosie had to fight tears back.

"I'm fine, baby," she lied. She wasn't fine. She was as mad as a cut snake and terrified of her power, but she wasn't about to let that show. "Just look at your shirt. Here," she began to use her leaf to scrape the egg off Maggie's top, and between them, they managed to clean up as best they could.

It would have been easier to take Maggie home after

that and reassess how they were going to tackle the vicious neighborhood gossips that seemed to circle overhead like vultures. But Rosie refused to let the lesser assets of Backwards USA get her down when she had already braved Randy's anger by leaving him. They continued the walk into town, Rosie's arm slung over her daughter's shoulder, and Maggie's little arm tucked protectively around her mother's waist.

"THEY *EGGED* YOU?" BEN ASKED AS HE BROUGHT PAPER towels out from behind the counter and started to rip wads off. "Entitled little shits," he said, and then as he handed the paper towels to Maggie, "Excuse my language, sweetheart. But man! That kind of behavior just—" He glanced at Maggie again and pushed his lips together, then looked back at Rosie with a whispered "- makes me so damn mad!"

He pointed at Rosie as he walked to wet a wad of paper towels in the sink. "You should report it to the Sheriff's Department. Here." He held out the wet towels, and Rosie accepted it gratefully. She began to wipe the sticky remnants of the egg off the side of her face, dampening and smoothing it over her long brown hair.

"There's no point," Rosie conceded. "There never is in towns like this. And besides, the whole town has it out for me."

"Not the whole town." Ben consoled her.

Rosie scoffed. "Well, a good portion of it!"

"It's only because you're the new girl in town," Ben said, crossing his arms over his chest. "Soon enough, people are gonna get to knowin' and acceptin' you," he promised. "Just you wait'n see."

That comment was the trigger.

"You know," Rosie said, her irritation leveling out into full-on anger. She put her free hand on her hip and gripped the broom with the other. "Since coming here, I've been spied on, hit on, been shunned by townsfolk, and had eggs thrown at me." She took a breath, trying to get her temper under control before she said something she would regret. "So, with all due respect Ben, your down-home views on Mosswood don't really gel with *my* personal experiences so far."

He blinked, a pink tinge coloring his cheeks as his eyes settled on anywhere but her. She hadn't meant to call him out that way, and she already wished she hadn't. He was still her boss, and she'd just jumped down his throat.

He looked over at Maggie, who was standing a little way away, trying to pretend she wasn't listening to the adults. He reached into his pocket and pulled out a stack of quarters.

"Here," he said, holding out the change to Maggie. "Why don't you go play some Pac-Man while I talk to your mom."

"Awesome!" Maggie hurried over to the retro video game as though frightened Ben would change his mind.

Ben met Rosie's gaze, holding his hand up in an expression of surrender. "You're right," he said. "I don't know about your struggles, Rosie. And I know I told you to keep the drama away from work, but I hope you know I'm always here to lend an ear if you need one." He shrugged. "I was new in town once, too."

Rosie sighed, holding the limp towels in front of her. "I'm sorry," she said. "I shouldn't take it out on you."

"It's okay," Ben told her with casual ease, leaning his butt against the counter. "You're only human, Rosie."

She snorted with a breath of wry laughter as she folded over the damp towels. "Don't feel it, lately," she confessed in a small voice.

Ben tilted his head as he looked at her. "You look like you got the weight of the world on your shoulders. Everything alright?"

Rosie huffed a breath out and then shook her head. "No."

Ben paused as though uncertain of himself before he spoke. "You wanna tell me what happened up at your cottage?" He peered at Rosie in a friendly but probing manner. "I mean, what really happened. With Terry?"

Rosie sighed and recounted the story. It felt good to have at least one person know the truth, that she wasn't the man-snatching home wrecker Tammy and Prissy wanted everyone to believe she was.

"Well, just as well Tammy found out now about her husband. Sorry it had to involve you," Ben said, frowning. "You're right, though. Reportin' the egging wouldn't do a fat lot a good. Sheriff Holt is Terry's brother."

She snorted and rolled her eyes. "Great." Then a thought occurred to her, and she narrowed her eyes at Ben. "You knew Terry wasn't faithful to Tammy?"

"Not 'knew,'" he replied. He stood and searched through a cabinet, then returned with an opened chocolate bar that looked like it might have been part of his lunch. Rosie took it as he continued in explanation. "But I've seen his roamin' eyes, if not his roamin' hands, if you know what I mean."

He brushed his palms onto his jeans. "He'd better watch himself. The only person in this town more popular than Tammy is the pastor, and if he didn't have a direct line to the big guy upstairs, I'm not sure even he would stand a chance."

Rosie pressed her lips together in a thin line and then took a bite of her chocolate. "Thanks," she said. "It's nice to know that not everyone in Mosswood is willing to tar me with the same brush."

"It took a long while for me to be accepted here, too," he admitted. "But I did get accepted. Eventually." He stood straighter. "Be careful what you wish for, though—once you're one of us, there's no such thing as privacy or personal space."

Rosie smiled. "Dunno that there's much of that now."

"Oh, it gets worse," he assured her. "Just you wait."

REVENGE WAS AT THE FOREFRONT OF ROSIE'S MIND AS she started her shift. Rosie knew that Prissy wasn't a fan of hers, but thinking that she would raise a son who threw eggs at a child made Rosie's blood boil. After completing all the usual start-of-shift chores, Rosie settled in behind the register. When an older man approached her to deliver a stack of neatly folded papers, Rosie knew what form her revenge would take.

The man paid without making eye contact and hurried out of the door, leaving her with the papers he had stacked on the counter—several newly minted copies of that month's *Herald of Hope Magazine*. And there, on the front cover in full color-printed glory (again), was Pastor Bishop with his wife and son leading the charge at the last Church event.

Rosie didn't even hesitate. She snatched the black pen from the top of the register's keyboard and started to give Prissy a creative makeover. The scribbled-on beard was over-the-top, but when combined with huge shaggy eyebrows, a hooked snout with a wart in place of Prissy's perfect, tiny nose and three blackened teeth-gaps, it all came together. Rosie was still scribbling when a shadow covered her handiwork, and she scrambled to cover the Prissy-monster she'd created.

Declan was grinning down at her. "Nice," he crooned. "Didn't realize you're an artist."

Rosie could feel herself blushing. Declan leaned forward, resting his forearms on the counter. It was clear that he was expecting an explanation, and she didn't know what to tell him. She avoided his gaze. She slipped the newsletter off the counter, folding it in half so that her artwork was on the inside.

"What's up?" he prompted her.

She sighed. Declan was the best friend she had right now. He'd helped her out with chores, set up the protective magic, been there for Maggie. Rosie bit the inside of her cheek as she weighed her options. The truth will set you free, right?

"Maggie and I got egged on our way into town this morning."

"What?"

"Egged," she repeated, glancing over at where Maggie was enthralled with Pac-Man and lowering her voice. "It's where someone drives past you and—"

"I know what it means. I just can't believe that someone in this town thinks they can get away with doing that to you and Maggie."

The protective tone of his voice made Rosie's shoulders relax and her cheeks threaten to turn up in a smile. But she didn't want him to think that she needed him to turn vigilante on the residents of Mosswood.

"I'm only going to tell you about what happened if you promise not to do anything about it," she warned him. "I'm telling you to get your advice and support, not so you can run off looking to be my knight in shining armor. Agreed?"

Declan's eyes roamed her face. She could see the scales in his mind weighing things, torn between wanting to support her and make whoever did this pay for it. At long last, he gave her a curt nod. "Agreed."

"Good." Rosie stood tall, feeling like it might give her the strength to tell the story from the beginning.

She told him about what happened the afternoon Terry had come by her place, and how it had devolved into the neighborhood having it out for her. Declan listened with a face of stone. Rosie didn't know whether his sudden seriousness made him look more handsome, or more imposing. She settled on the latter, and as she drew to the end of her story, she eyed him warily.

"That's it," she finished.

Declan stared at her. It wasn't the same kind of lingering look he'd given her before, where his eyes had traveled over her nose, lips, throat, and then back to her eyes. There was no cocky gleam in his eyes, no smirk hovering on his lips. He looked ready to rumble, and Rosie worried that he would break his promise and rampage through the town, cracking skulls as he went.

And she couldn't say that the thought was unappealing.

"I see," he said finally.

Silence crept between them. The store was empty except for them and Maggie, and things would be slow. Rosie watched Declan's face for signs of life, but when he gave nothing away, she had to take the bait.

"You see?" she asked, shocked. "That's all you have to say?"

He met her gaze then, and she could see the tortured look in his eyes.

"No. That's not even close to being fuckin' *all,*" he growled. His hands curled into tight fists on the counter-top, and she could feel the air crackling with energy around him.

"Why have yeh let the people in this shithole town treat yeh so badly? To the point where they think it's okay to throw eggs at you and your wee'an?"

"Me?" she asked, before lowering her voice to a furious whisper. "You're blaming *me* for someone throwing eggs at me?"

He flustered, looking around the front of the store as though he might find something there to help him express his feelings. When he failed, he flapped his arms by his side.

"Of course, it's not *your* fault you got egged," he said in a hushed voice. "But why haven't you reported it to the Sheriff or something? What if that egg had hit you or Maggie in the eye? One or both of you could have been seriously hurt. Nobody treats you like this and gets away with it!"

"Because the Sheriff is Terry's brother!" Rosie

exclaimed a little louder than she had meant to. "So, what's the damn point? And they *didn't* get away with it. I was so mad after it happened, I used magic to explode the eggs they still had all over their car."

Declan paused in his rant and then laughed, the kind that said he was trying to hold it in, but it burst out through closed lips anyway. "So, you... you egged them back?"

She tilted her head to look at him. "Yes! I egged them back! I know they're stupid kids who threw eggs at me, but what if it had hit *them* in the eye? They were driving! What if they ran off the road or into oncoming traffic?"

Declan sobered, and she lifted her eyebrows. "I'm not in control of my magic, and I need to be." She looked down at the counter, over at her daughter, and then back up at him. "What if *I* hurt Maggie?"

He let out a long breath, nodding as the realization of what Rosie was saying settled around him. "You're right," he told her. "We do need to work on getting your magic under control. You've already shown so much promise, what with fixin' the window and redoing the wards around the cottage. I guess I lost sight of the fact that you're still new at this."

He reached out, his hand coming to rest on her shoulder before he squeezed it. "I'm sorry."

"Well, good," Rosie said. Her emotions were a tangled snarl of confusion, excitement, anger, fear, and hope. They all shoved against one another, and she wasn't sure which of them she was supposed to let herself feel first. "I only just found out that I'm a witch. It's too much to ask that I just happen to know *how* to be one without a little help!"

"We'll work on it together," he promised, rubbing his hand on her upper arm. Rosie found herself leaning into his touch. "But something *has* to be done about this neighborhood vendetta against you. You need to feel safe, and that shit's not cool."

"I know," Rosie admitted, before holding her hands up in a placating gesture. "But I told you I will handle it. Okay? All of it. Things like this need to be done delicately, or else I could be run out of town." She took a breath, her voice dropping to a murmur. "And we don't have anywhere else to go."

"I know the feeling," he admitted. His expression softened when he glanced at her, and he shook his head. "Promise me that if anything *else* like this happens, you'll tell me?"

Rosie quirked a brow, which hitched itself even higher when Declan added "Please," to the end of his request.

"Okay," she agreed. She ran her hands through her long coffee-colored locks and began to scoop it up into a ponytail, more for something to do than because it was annoying her. "At least I haven't heard anything else from Randy or his cronies." She looped her hair through the elastic band she usually kept on her wrist for that purpose. "Thankfully."

A shadow passed over Declan's face, and he cleared his throat. "Yeah, we'll count our blessings," he said, straightening. "I better get these deliveries off the truck and into the dock."

Rosie blinked. "You came in to see me before you'd even unloaded?"

Declan's trademark cheek came flooding back onto his face as though a dam had broken. "There's a comment in there somewhere about unloading that's dirty and socially unacceptable, that would make ya blush and hit me if I uttered it," he told her.

Rosie shrugged. "But you're a gentleman and not gonna go there... right?"

He was still chuckling as he started for the door.

"I'll give you a hand," she offered, following him. "Not like I'm inundated with customers."

"Great," he called back to her. "Thanks, love."

If Rosie didn't know better, she would have sworn that he fell into a swagger, once he knew she was following behind her. And then she realized, she did know better, and he definitely *was* swaggering for her. She smirked and rolled her eyes because the antic was so utterly Declan that she couldn't help but find it a little funny. And then there was the flip side, where she had to admit to herself that the man filled out a pair of jeans way too well

They began unloading the trays of fruit and vegetables from the bed of the truck. Rosie couldn't help noticing the way the muscles in his arms bunched and moved as he shifted the crates or the way that he caught her noticing every single time she dared to sneak a peek.

But the expected taunt about her 'seeing something she liked' didn't come, and that surprised her even more than her growing interest in Declan's biceps. After all, it wasn't a crime to appreciate a hot guy. And the more she thought about, the more Rosie was starting to think that hot wasn't all he was.

She grabbed one of the last trays, immediately regretting picking up the potatoes instead of the lettuce. She stepped over to the side of the truck bed and onto the dock, where Declan was coming back from a return trip. She shuffled to the left, her fingers white with effort on the handles of the tray. Declan followed before they both ducked right to pass. She smiled and huffed a small laugh, and then felt Declan's fingers close over hers.

"Here," he offered, slipping his hands around and then under her grip. "Allow me."

She watched him, her eyes wide, as he took the weight from her. She let her hands linger, fingers over his now as he shifted to take the tray with ease. He glanced down, looking at their hands entwined, before meeting her gaze.

"Thanks," was all she could manage to say.

The hint of a smile—a kind smile, and not his signature smirk—came and went. His face was solemn as he leaned forward, his eyes skipping down to her lips as she realized that he was about to—

"There you are!"

Ben stood in the doorway that led back into the store, smiling at both of them in a way that said his morning off had left him well-rested.

"Sorry!" Rosie blurted, stepping back from Declan. She brushed her hands down the front of her skinny jeans as though it might rid them of the warm, tingling sensation left there by Declan's touch. "Are there customers waiting?"

"No," Ben said in a slow drawl, looking between Declan and Rosie as though he was trying to come to the right conclusion but was missing a few vital clues. "I just wondered where you were. Hey, Declan—do you have a sec? I was hoping to go over next week's inventory with you."

"Grand," Declan replied a touch too quickly, and Rosie glanced at him out the corner of her eye. She was glad to know that she wasn't the only one embarrassed by their moment on the loading dock.

"Rosie," he added, following Ben inside, "are you okay unloading those last two crates?"

"Sure." She turned to step back onto the truck, where the lettuce and celery awaited her. She was about to get the sack trolley so that she could take the delivery inside when she heard a strange sound. Like a particularly musical cricket chirping. In the middle of a parking lot?

She froze for a moment, straining to hear it. And when she turned her head in the direction of the cab of

Declan's truck, she realized it was his phone. Trotting over to the passenger door, Rosie bent and reached through the open window to retrieve the cell.

She hadn't meant to spy what was on his phone preview, but it was difficult not to notice the gigantic letters above the green and red phone icons on the screen. *Father.* So formal. She tried to back out of the window but got stuck—she wasn't as young as she used to be—and before she could make her exit, she accidentally spied on him again.

The phone stopped ringing, and then after, a text message quickly popped up.

'Any progress?'

She frowned and shimmied back out of the window, clutching the phone in one hand, and turned to find Declan standing behind her.

"Oh," she breathed. "Sorry, I—I just heard your phone ringing, and I thought it might be important, so I was going to run it in to you and... and—"

"And you thought you'd have a sticky-beak in my truck?" he asked, and the tone was so unusual for him that Rosie blinked.

"No! I mean, I saw. But..." she floundered, and then she shrugged, as though to give up on any of the excuses she could have plucked from thin air. "Is everything okay?" she asked him instead.

"Not really," he told her. "But it's not your problem."

She narrowed her eyes at him, annoyed that it was okay for her to share her problems with him, but that it didn't seem to be a two-way street. "Fine," she said, shoving his phone into his chest. "Your dad called."

"You looked in my phone, too?" he raised his voice after her as she retreated.

"Don't flatter yourself, moron," she called back, heading for the counter. "It was on the screen."

CHAPTER TWELVE

A s the afternoon wore on, Rosie could feel her funk settling heavier around her shoulders, like the arm of a shoulder-devil cuddling her closer for a pep talk. Every time she heard a noise coming from the back of the store, she turned, hoping to see Declan striding through the loading dock door with a delivery. When he didn't appear, the thundercloud over her head darkened a little more.

When the front doors whooshed open, Rosie looked up out of habit to see who had entered. Prissy Bishop pranced into the store, dressed in a pale pink suit more suited to the first lady than to a pastor's wife. She stomped straight up to the counter and tore off her enormous sunglasses to glare at her, but Rosie was distracted.

It looked like the woman was wearing some kind of extreme Halloween makeup. Her eyebrows were beyond bushy and puffed out in such a way that made it look like she had a sloping caveman's forehead. Rosie's eyes widened as she took in the deep wrinkles around Prissy's face, and when she spoke, Rosie could have sworn that a few of her teeth looked like they were black and rotten.

Just the way she had sketched her on the Church magazine cover!

"There is raw egg all over the interior of my son's car," Prissy snarled, "and I'd like to know how you're planning on fixin' it!"

Resisting the urge to laugh, Rosie blinked and leaned back, as though it would help her get a better perspective of the situation.

"Hold up," she said, holding out a hand to stave off any further outbursts from Prissy. "What you're saying to me is you know your son egged my ten-year-old daughter and me, but you're mad because he has raw egg in his upholstery?"

Prissy opened her mouth to retort, and then covered her mouth with her hand to hide her teeth. "I'm mad because he didn't put raw egg all over his *own* car!" Prissy pursed her lips and reached up to resettle her huge sunglasses on the bridge of her unusually crooked nose.

"I don't follow," Rosie replied. "What exactly do you think I did to make eggs explode in your son's car? From where I was standing on the highway with my daughter, dripping with eggs your son threw at us?"

While Prissy seemed to need a little time to muster up a reply, Rosie saw an opportunity to set things straight, and she took it.

"I oughta report this to the Sheriff's Department," she mused. "I'll bet that at least one of the shops on the highway – probably Granny's—has security footage of your son driving past us. And I have witnesses who saw us arrive here for my shift covered in egg." She gave a tiny false sigh. "What *will* people think when they find out how Pastor Bishop's kid acts towards his neighbors."

It was clear from the look on the other woman's face that this altercation wasn't going the way she had planned it. Prissy faltered, and an idea struck Rosie. She might not be able to change the way people in Mosswood treated her, but she could deter any further eggings *and* get some chores done.

"Of course, I'd much prefer to be able to handle this between ourselves like grown women, if you can stand to act like one."

The doors of the Go-Go-Mart slid open to admit Declan, who took one glance at the two women and wisely opted to go towards the back of the store to check Maggie's score on Pac-Man instead.

Prissy was too spooked to speak. She stuffed her sunglasses back onto her face and darted for the exit. Just as she made it to the automatic doors, she turned to look back.

"I'll pray for you, Rosie," she huffed, before flouncing out onto the sidewalk.

Rosie let go of a breath she hadn't realized she'd been holding, fighting back the urge to grin at the memory of Prissy's face.

She glanced at Declan. His usually unruly red locks were swept to one side in a style that was reminiscent of 1930s glamor, and his typical lumberjack-esque attire had been replaced with well-fitted chinos and a crisp pale blue shirt. He looked terrific, and Rosie fought against her primal urge to drink in the sight of him.

All the many things she had wanted to say to him flew out of her brain, leaving her mouth dry. Instead of any of the witty greetings she had contrived, what her sluggish reflexes finally decided to go with was a hesitant wave.

His brows flickered with surprise, but he went with it and offered her a half-hearted wave back. And then he turned his attention back to Pac-Man.

LIFE FELT SO MUCH MORE COMPLICATED THAT afternoon, as she and Maggie rode home beside Declan in his big rickety truck. The windows were rolled low enough for the wind to tug at her ponytail, almost drowning out the awkward silence between Declan and herself. Maggie had looked between the two of them as the truck started out of town and decided her book would be better company for the ride home.

As the truck pulled up the drive, Rosie felt her stomach turn as she took in the sight of the cottage itself. It looked as though a tornado had hit; the mailbox was knocked clear to the ground, mail and the pages of a newspaper littering the yard. Deep tire marks ran in huge rings over the lawn and through Rosie's restored flower beds. The bay window in the front of the house stood intact, but the others were shattered. The front door had been kicked in below the handle, splintering even though the deadlock had held. And spray-painted in bright red letters from across the front of the cottage from one side to the other were two huge words.

STUPIDBITCH

Rosie gasped, then felt all the air whoosh out of her lungs. She turned to pull Maggie to her as Declan parked the truck, trying to stop her daughter from seeing the worst of the carnage, but Maggie struggled and craned her neck for a look. Declan's neutral expression had vanished, leaving a chill in the air of the truck's cab.

"You two wait here," he said in a tone that was less of a request and more of an order. "I *mean* it, Rosie— keep her in the truck and lock the doors once I'm out. I need to check that it's safe."

He needn't have asked her twice. If Maggie hadn't

been there, then wild horses wouldn't have been able to keep her in that damn truck, but there was no way she would risk Maggie's safety. Declan stepped down from the cab, and Rosie reached hastily to lock both doors.

Declan searched the garden and woods surrounding the cottage. After what seemed like forever, he came back around front, scaled the porch steps two at a time, and then busted the front door open the rest of the way with one powerful push-kick.

He must have been satisfied that the house was safe because he soon re-emerged onto the porch where Rosie could see, giving her a curt nod of approval. In a heartbeat, Rosie had unlocked the passenger door and jumped down onto the grass, holding her arms up to help Maggie. They walked hand in hand over the lawn to the porch and looked up at Declan.

"They're long gone," he growled. Rosie noticed that both of his hands were balled into huge, hammer-like fists. "The fu—nny-lookin' meanies," he finished, switching out the f-bomb to something more child-appropriate at the last second. "Alright, ladies?"

Rosie could still feel her heart rattling in her chest. The breathlessness that usually accompanied her arguments with Randy made her wheeze every time she took a gulp of air.

And that's when she saw it. Held up by a hunting knife stabbed into the wood of the porch hung a note with large, uneven handwriting.

"Oh, sh—oot," Declan said as he noticed what she

was staring at. Rosie tried to tear her gaze away and couldn't.

CAME TO SEE YOU BUT YOU WEREN'T HOME. WON'T BE LONG NOW. YOUR LOVING HUSBAND.

Declan was at her side in an instant, reading the note that she still held in her trembling gaze. "That bastard won't get near you or Maggie, I swear to you," he growled in a low tone meant for Rosie's ears only.

But Maggie proved that children are usually much brighter than the adults around them give them credit for.

"Dad did this, didn't he?" Both of them turned to look at her stricken little face, and Rosie nodded. "Why does he hate us so much?"

Rosie thought her heart would break, as her mini-me looked up at her with sadness in her big hazel eyes. She could have said it was because those types of people didn't have enough love in their lives to know how to be kind, or some other fluffy reason that would sugar-coat the situation. But none of those excuses were right, and after making excuses for Randy for years, Rosie was through.

"Because some people," Rosie said, "are just horrible people, Pumpkin. Some try to hide it, and some of 'em are real open about it. Sometimes there ain't no rhyme or reason for why they're like that—they just wanna hurt people, and they go out of their way to do it, too." She wrapped her arms around her daughter and hugged her. "But that doesn't mean that we have to be like them. Not now, not ever."

They shared a brief but fierce hug, and then they walked up the porch steps and through the front door.

"Is it safe for me to go to my room?" Maggie asked then.

He nodded. "Sure is, wee'an. Maybe it'd be a good idea if you stayed in there until your mother'n I clean up all these splinters and broken glass."

"Okay," Maggie agreed, bouncing back with the resilience of a child who was only glad she wasn't on clean up duty.

The porch was silent for a moment, even though the ghost of an ex-husband-not-quite-past still hung in the air. Rosie lifted her gaze to Declan.

"How did he break through the wards?" she asked. She didn't realize how much she had been relying on the promise of Declan's magic to protect her, or how much she had believed in it until that moment. But with her yard trashed and the home where Maggie slept broken around them, that trust was fading.

The look of wariness on Declan's face didn't help matters. "Means his intent was stronger than ours," he said.

Rosie felt her shoulders sink as she looked around them at the mess.

"Rosie," he interrupted her worrying. She looked up

at him, and he met her gaze. "You're goin' to have to redo the wards yourself."

She took another deep breath and looked around the yard. What choice did she have?

THIS TIME, ROSIE DIDN'T HESITATE TO STRIP. SHE SHED her clothes, determination building in the pit of her stomach as she stepped down onto the lawn and into the waning moonlight. Remembering that adage about the third time being the charm, she promised herself that this was it. Randy was *not* going to be able to bully his way through the wards this time around. She wasn't willing to accept that his intent to harm them was more potent than her intent to protect her child.

The nighttime chorus of insects and frogs soothed her as she strode towards the mailbox, where she stopped for a minute. She crouched down, placing both of her palms against the warm, damp earth. And then she remembered what Declan had said when he had taught her how to fix the window.

Rosie pushed her fingertips down into the soil, letting it surround her hands. The gritty dirt held traces of feeling – loss, hope, love. The emotions were little more than trace elements, diluted by years of emptiness and longing, but they were there. She took a deep breath as she sifted her fingers through them, making sure that she felt every single one in her heart before she let out her breath in a long, steady stream.

Into that breath, Rosie poured her *own* emotions. Her love for her daughter, first, followed by her desire to keep Maggie safe. A gut-churning hatred for Randy, and a determination to see his influence over their lives banished forever. Rosie's new-found strength, and the confidence that was blooming inside of her with each day that she took control of her own life back. The first kernels of peace she had experienced in years, owing all to the sanctuary of this small, rickety cottage in the woods.

She stood, letting the soil trickle through her fingers like beach sand until it was all gone, and there were only streaks of dirt left on her hands. Without knowing why she smeared a streak of the soil over her left breast, close to her heart, and then took up the last of her rock salt supply.

As she started to perform the ritual for the third time, she connected with the blanket of nature that settled around her shoulders as she moved. She wasn't' afraid her neighbors or Declan would see, and she wasn't scared that there was something in the shadows waiting to get her. *She* was the thing to be feared in these woods.

Once again, she trailed a thin line of salt behind her as she walked. And this time as the salt fell, it glowed a bright, iridescent turquoise as the earth absorbed her spell.

She hadn't wanted to return to the house yet. Putting her clothes back on had been the only concession she'd made. Knowing that the wards were as strong as she had the power to make them gave her a kind of peace that was liberating. For the first time since their arrival in Mosswood, Rosie slipped away without her daughter in tow. She walked barefoot through the woods, letting the trees whisper their soft stories to her until, at last, she came to the clearing where Declan's trailer was.

The rush of power she had felt as she wove the wards around the cottage was addictive. Magic-on-purpose was so different from magic-by-accident; there was a pure adrenaline surge associated. When she wandered into the clearing, her eyes settled on the charred places where tall grass and a ratty trailer had once stood.

And then she knew why she had come.

Framed by massive trees that trailed Spanish moss in the sweet summer breeze, the clearing was beautiful. The grass swayed like an ocean, a handful of fireflies dancing above their serene waves. And then there was the reminder of hate – of *cruelty* – burned right into the middle of this natural haven. Rosie stepped forward, her hands outstretched as she focused her will on the charred patch in the middle of the clearing.

She let the energy flow through her slowly at first, seeping from her fingertips in a gentle current. And then as she was able to direct it to the blackened grass, she let it flow more like a mighty river. Tiny spearheads of grass began to poke themselves up through the black-ened mess, bright green with hope. They soared upwards, becoming a tide of new growth that melted into the edges of the ocean of grass around it. Attracted by the energy, more fireflies drifted into the clearing. They danced across the air, and Rosie laughed breath-lessly, clapping her hands together in delight as the last of her spell left her.

"You're incredible," Declan said from behind her.

She spun to face him, her dark curls fanning around her with the movement. Her eyes were bright as she took in the sight of him, leaning against a tree at the edge of the woods with his hands tucked in his pockets. An expression of pure wonder was painted across his face, and Rosie's smile widened as she let the elation of her successful magic wash over her.

"I know, right?" she laughed, punch-drunk on the feeling. "Who'd a thunk it?"

He pushed off the tree and walked towards her, a soft smile on his face. The grass brushed against the bottoms of his jeans as he moved, and she let her gaze roam over him as he came closer.

"I did," he murmured, reaching out as though to stroke her cheek. A firefly darted between them, making them both jump and laugh. But as their laughter and smiles faded into the warm air surrounding them, an altogether more serious atmosphere descended.

The void between them seemed filled with some-thing unseen. It was the humming of their individual energies—their magical forces—reaching out to one another. She was surprised to feel how intense it was, and for a moment, she let the throbbing sensation of his energy mingling with hers overwhelm her.

When she met his gaze, he was staring down at her with pure, unabashed desire. Rosie's breath caught in her throat, and a small voice in the back of her mind reminded her that she was supposed to be working. But a raw wilderness in her soul wound its tendrils around her heart and squeezed.

She tilted her chin up towards him, willing him to kiss her. It was the only invitation he needed. His arms pulled her tight against the length of his whole body, which would have been enough sensation to explore on its own, but then his lips met hers in a hot, demanding kiss, and she lost herself to the experience. He tasted like the sweet whiskey scent she had come to associate with him, and his tongue teased hers into becoming bolder, to match his efforts as the kiss deepened.

Her hands reached into his hair, pulling his mouth back to hers after they broke for a ragged intake of breath. Rosie gave her heart and soul to that kiss, not realizing that it had been waiting there for release since the moment she had seen him wander up to the cottage in the darkness the first night they'd met.

CHAPTER THIRTEEN

Rosie should have felt more in control of the situation. The wards on the cottage had been re-established. She was gaining a better handle on her magic in general. But she hadn't been able to settle all week, and she wasn't sure whether it was because she was stressing about the possibility of Randy coming back or because of her blooming magical powers. Is this just what it felt like to become a witch?

The sight of Mosswood nestled in the valley below The Ridge calmed her as she washed the day's dishes ahead of her evening shift. A subtle noise behind her alerted her to Declan joining her, and he picked up a dishtowel to dry as she washed.

"You can feel it, can't ya?" he asked.

She paused in her washing, looking at him sharply. "You mean it's a real thing? I thought I was just PMSing or something!"

He ignored her sass, swiping the dish towel over a plate. "It's a forebodin'—an energy shift. You can feel it in the air. Trouble's comin'."

His words picked at the unraveling thread of her inner fears. "Is it Randy?"

"I'm a witch, not a psychic," he sassed her back, with a tight smile.

"Don't tell me *psychics* are real, too."

She took a deep breath. Ever since Declan had arrived, she had felt in over her head. She had tumbled head over heels into a world that she still didn't know anything about. And the further she fell down the rabbit-hole, it seemed like the more there was to know.

Declan misinterpreted her silence for a different kind of anxiety. "It's nothin' to worry about. We've taken all the proper precautions."

She thought of the stronger wards and the ring and necklace that she and Maggie both wore now. And then she narrowed her eyes at him. "Why didn't you think to tell me that there was a forbidden shift coming?"

"A foreboding," he corrected her, taking care to pronounce the 'ing' around his accent. "S'no point in worryin' ya ahead a'time."

"Well, I'm gonna worry whether you tell me or not," she huffed, passing him the last dish to dry. "At least if you bothered to keep me in the loop, I'd know what to expect – in a way."

She wrung the dishcloth out into the sink. "How do we even know that our precautions will work? I mean, you said it yourself. His intent was that much stronger than ours before. What if he breaks through mine?"

"This is exactly why I didn't tell ya about the foreboding," he replied, glancing at her out of the corner of his eye.

Rosie turned to face him, her hand resting on the sink. "Well, I just want to be as prepared as we can be if he's coming for us!"

"You know him better than me," Declan told her. "Do you think we're prepared?"

Rosie's stomach flipped over itself as she considered the depth of the question. Did she feel ready to take Randy on, once and for all?

"I don't think anyone really knows him," she said at last, crossing her arms over her belly to calm it. "He's barely even human anymore."

Declan hung up the drying cloth and turned to envelop Rosie into a tight, comforting hug. One of his arms slipped around her waist to draw her close, and his other hand curled protectively around the back of her head. He pressed a quick kiss to the top of her head.

"We'll do the best we can, then," he murmured into her hair.

They spent the afternoon testing the wards on the property boundary and imposing new wards on the cottage itself while Maggie read inside. By the time dinner rolled around, Rosie and Declan were exhausted. They sat at the small round table with Maggie, who pushed her beans around on her plate before she glanced up at her mom.

"Today feels weird," she declared, dropping her fork on the table so that she could rub a small hand across her forehead. "Like... the air is heavy. And I'm tired from the crazy dream I had last night."

Rosie watched her daughter, careful not to let any kind of panic show on her face. "Yeah, it's been pretty humid today," she said, even though she knew good and well that's not what Maggie had meant. "What were your dreams about, Pumpkin?"

"Just random stuff," Maggie sighed, going back to her dinner. Rosie took a chance and glanced at Declan, who was watching Maggie with veiled concern.

"A nice warm glass of milk might help you sleep better tonight," he said, polishing off his mashed potatoes and moving to dunk a biscuit in his gravy.

"Okay," Maggie said in a low voice that was so different from her usual chipper buzz that Rosie felt her heart squeeze with worry. She met Declan's eyes across the table, but neither of them said anything else.

EARLY EVENING WAS ROSIE'S FAVORITE TIME OF DAY AT the cottage. The wind tickled the chime she'd hung up outside on the front porch, and the crickets sang their slow, sweet lullabies. She liked sitting on the porch with a glass of wine to relax after a hard day. It wasn't until she'd taken up residence on the porch swing that she realized tonight was the first time she'd had company for her evening reverie.

Declan was almost sheepish as he stepped through the front door and onto the porch, his eyes darting to her glass of wine and then to meet her gaze. Rosie glanced up at him, her drink at her lips. She sipped, letting her eyes coast down over his broad chest before looking away.

"Mind if I join you?"

He sounded amused and didn't wait for her answer before he lowered himself onto the porch swing next to her. It groaned under his weight as he leaned back, and it swung out with the motion. Rosie tried to steady her wine, and once the swing had lulled into a slow roll, she looked at him.

"By all means," she said at last, good-natured sarcasm coloring her words. It felt good to have someone—an adult—to joke and shoot the breeze with.

Declan smirked. "You're too kind." He slipped a hand into his inside jacket pocket and drew out a small, full bottle of whiskey. With a smooth, expert motion, he cracked open the lid and took a swig. Rosie expected the obligatory 'ah!' That usually accompanied people's attempts to drink straight liquor, but none came. She side-eyed him as he took another swig of booze like it was mother's milk.

"What are you, some kind of alcoholic?"

"Actually," Declan began, feigning indignation, "I

don't drink all that much." He paused a beat, pretending to reconsider his statement. "Or is it 'I don't drink all that often'? Either way," he tilted his bottle towards her glass and chinked them together companionably. "Cheers."

Rosie rolled her eyes and shook her head, but one side of her mouth twitched into a smirk.

"See how easy it is?" he asked her, turning to gaze out across the moonlit lawn that swept down towards the road.

"How easy what is?" She watched him for a moment.

His gaze wandered over the trees that swallowed the driveway, up to the almost-full moon, before drifting back to meet hers.

"How easy it is to let Fate have her way."

Rosie scoffed and took another sip, swallowing before answering. "Fate... or you?"

He shrugged, another weapon in his arsenal of casual charm. "Can't help it if my goals align with hers every once in a while," he smiled.

"And what *are* your goals, exactly?"

He hesitated for a split second, but a shadow passed over his face.

"To marry my Queen. To protect my people."

It was her turn to hesitate. Even the crickets' song dipped into a lull as a light breeze rushed through the trees. This was the first time he'd mentioned anything about his home. There was something in his tone that sounded sad.

He leaned back in the swing, his head resting on the back of the chair, and his chin tilted up towards the sky. His face was in profile against the moonlight, and it gave him an otherworldly appearance that had Rosie staring at him.

She couldn't say he was conventionally handsome. His nose was too large and too crooked, and his eyes were a little too close together. But as he turned his head so that he could look over at her, she could see the fullness of his lips and his strong jaw balanced the nose out well, and there was a look of hope in his eyes that made her want to lean in close to him.

The sound of a creature calling in the woods broke the spell that had begun to weave itself between them. Rosie looked away, lifting her wine to her lips to prevent them from being tempted to press up against his.

In that unflappable way of his, Declan seemed entirely at ease. He watched her gulp her wine, eyes lingering on the lips that had contemplated betraying her.

"And what is it that *you* want, Rosie?" he asked.

She didn't even have to think about it. "Peace and quiet," Rosie sighed, leaning back on the swing next to him. "It's all I've ever wanted. Ever since I could remember."

He snorted and nodded at the moon as though they

were sharing an inside joke. And then he stretched his arm along the back of the swing behind her, rocking them in the swing.

"Good luck, love," he told her with a chuckle. "Haven't ya heard that sayin'? Heavy lies the head that wears the crown."

"No." She frowned, not liking the sound of it. "I haven't. What's it from?"

Declan nodded again. "Shakespeare or somethin'. Pay heed—" he pointed at her with his bottle, "—Peace ain't for the likes of us."

She narrowed her eyes at him, annoyance rising in her.

"All I want is to protect *my* people, too—Maggie and me—from Randy, from selfish townspeople, and from anyone else who cares more about their own goals than they do about us." She glanced down at her wine and then shook her head. "I grew up with chaos. She's getting better."

"You don't think I want that for her?" Declan asked, face suddenly angry.

She snorted a laugh. "I don't think you've given any thought to that at all." She gestured at him. "You showed up on my front porch drunk as a skunk that first night. Did you think about Maggie then? About what men drinking around her might have meant to her when we lived with Randy?"

Declan had the good sense to look chagrined and retreated his arm back across the swing.

She looked him in the eyes. "I'm willing to sacrifice *everything* to make up for the first ten years of lost peace I caused that child. And if you stand in the way of that, your people will just have to stay queen-less, fate or no."

Rosie drained the rest of her wine and stood. "I'm off to bed," she announced, starting up the lawn. "Try not to snore."

"Only if you promise to do the same, Your Majesty," he threw back at her.

CHAPTER FOURTEEN

Rosie woke with a head full of fog the next morning. She'd heard every little sound through the night, tossing and turning, until the birdsong in the woods woke her just before dawn. She lay in bed for a while, not wanting to have to deal with Declan so early. But coffee called to her. She scowled and threw off her sheet in childish defiance. Then she got dressed and tiptoed into the kitchen, checked on Maggie, and took her coffee out to the porch without bothering to make Declan one.

The air was already hot and humid, but a slight breeze promised a lazy summer afternoon. Rosie sat on the top porch step and surveyed her damaged garden beds, the tire marks through the lawn, and the flattened mailbox she hadn't yet set right. It felt as though all she did was take one step forward and two steps back, and it was a pattern she was getting tired of. But if she didn't keep taking those steps forward, Randy would win. And she was tired of Randy winning.

From her perch in the sun, Rosie focused her mind on the mailbox, pushing her energy out so that she could lift it from its sad bed in the dirt. She didn't stop there. She refreshed the peeling white paint on the box, closing her eyes to envision bright red letters spelling out 'BELL' on the side. As she poured her magic into restoring the mailbox, the overflow drifted down to the ground beneath it. Bright green shoots appeared in a clump around the base of the mailbox, growing and lengthening until they were long strappy leaves that gave way to lush blooms of yellow-centered jonquils.

Rosie beamed, watching the flowers nod their heads in the breeze. She didn't want to stop there. Everything that Randy and his men had wrecked with their brutality, she would mend with magic from within herself. The lawn was next, springing up thicker and lusher than it had been before. The dirt in the garden beds scurried back to where it belonged, and then she repaired the flowers that had been damaged in the carnage.

As she sat back and rested the heels of her hands on the new deck of the porch behind her, Rosie felt a deep sense of self-satisfaction wash over her. She was building a home here for her and Maggie. Her eyes wandered over the repaired garden, taking in the ancient oak tree in the middle of the yard, the late summer blooms sharing their fragrance, and the beautiful periwinkle vine that grew around the porch railing.

She guessed a little to-ing and fro-ing made it all worthwhile.

But Rosie's admiration of her handiwork was short-lived. The tell-tale growl of noisy motorcycles on the road out front set her heart racing. One Harley came into view around the bend, stout and imposing, and it chilled the blood in her veins. It was followed by several more.

Randy had found her.

She leaped to her feet as they pulled up, and though inside she was terrified, she refused to show it. Several large, tattooed men with long hair got off the bikes and began to stroll towards her like they owned the place. The one most in front was smaller than the others, grayer, and had a potbelly, but the rest of them didn't seem to care that he was the least physically impressive of the bunch.

"Well now *here* you are, Rosie," Randy called across the lawn. He leaned to the side to spit tobacco onto the jonquils she had just grown beneath her shiny new mailbox. "Good to see you're keepin' well. Been awful worried 'bout ya."

She gave a disbelieving snort and tucked her arms across her chest so that he wouldn't be able to see her balled fists. With all the brainpower she could muster, she prayed that Maggie would stay inside, but it was unlikely. A herd of Harleys pulling into a place was sort of hard to miss.

"Find that a little hard to believe," she shot back

with false bravado. "Only thing you ever cared about is who's cleaning up your messes."

"Suppose that's why I'm here," Randy growled. "Don't like having no unfinished business trailin' me."

"I'm not unfinished business." Rosie squared her jaw, watching them get closer. "I'm none of your business at all. Not anymore. And neither is Maggie."

Randy grinned. "Now, now, babe. We both know the sooner you collect up our baby girl and get on back to Atlanta, the easier this'll be on everyone."

The men were all standing at the front of the property, and Rosie wondered if it was because the wards prevented them from venturing any closer. She didn't want to take the chance and was desperate for cover. Taking a slow step back, she tried to calculate the distance between herself and her front door.

"Y'know," a familiar lilting voice called out then, ringing out from behind Randy and his crew. "I've never seen apes wearing leather before."

Declan was leaning against the side of Randy's motorcycle. His arms were crossed, his broad shoulders giving him the appearance of a Viking, with biceps that looked like they needed their own zip codes. His huge boots planted in the dirt with authority, and he squinted at the men, taunting them with an arrogant smirk.

"I wouldn't say it's altogether flatterin', lads."

"Who the fuck are you?" the biggest biker, a man with a long bleach-blonde mullet snarled, "and where the *hell* d'you come from?"

It was an excellent question—Rosie was looking in that direction, and she hadn't seen Declan arrive either. Declan's answer was a slow, measured grin.

"I'm ya worst fuckin' nightmare," he replied, "and that's all you need t'know 'bout it."

"This ain't got nothin' to do with you, Red," Blondie warned.

"That's where ya wrong, mate," Declan's grin seemed calm, but he looked past the bikers to meet Rosie's gaze. There was something in that look that made her want to hold her breath, and she tried to call out to him that it wasn't worth it, but he beat her to the punch.

"It's got *everythin'* to do with me."

With that, the men charged back down the lawn at him and away from the wards. He remained perched on the seat of the bike, casually watching them pelting his way. The big guy was the first to reach him, lunging for Declan as soon as he was close enough.

Declan's leg shot out like a snake striking its prey, his huge boot crunching into the middle of the guy's face. Incandescent blue light sparked between them as Declan's foot came away. Rosie gaped, wondering if she had seen that happen. She didn't have to wonder for long, though, because Blondie had grabbed Declan's arm and yanked him off the motorcycle.

The huge Irishman hit the dirt with a pronounced thud, but he didn't let the fall hinder him. He swept his right arm wide in a long arc, connecting with the side of Blondie's knee. A sickening crack reached Rosie on the porch, and she flinched as Blondie cried out in pain. Another bolt of electricity zap between Declan and Blondie as he tumbled to the ground. Pain and instinct should have seen the guy cradling his knee, which Rosie had no doubt was broken. But instead, he lay on his side in the fetal position, convulsing.

Declan had sat up on the lawn, his eyes seeking her out. His gaze met hers as she watched on from the porch, and though he looked fine—even as though he was enjoying this a bit—she could tell that he was worried for her. And then the third biker, the guy who had been closest to Randy, reached him and put him in a chokehold.

"Hey!" she yelled, leaping off the porch and running across the lawn towards Declan. But Randy got in her way, and this time he had pulled out his massive handgun.

Rosie skidded to a halt, her eyes darting to the mailbox and then back to Randy. She was still inside the wards.

"What the hell do you want?" she asked, her worried gaze darting to Declan, who was struggling against the biker's hold around his neck.

"I want my family back, Rosie," Randy cooed at her. "Ain't that obvious? I want my house in Atlanta to have my kid in it. I want my favorite meal cookin' on the stove, and I want my wife there to suck my dick when I *fuckin' tell her to!*" The last four words were screamed, spittle flying from his mouth.

"I'm not comin' back," Rosie said, forcing herself to take a deep breath and standing her ground even when Randy swung the gun to aim it at her head. "And neither is Maggie. I'm done letting you treat me like a piece of meat and letting her see it and think that's what marriage is. I'm done letting you ignore her. I'm done letting you put your shit on us and think you can get away with it."

"Well, that just breaks my heart, darlin'," Randy said. "I guess that means we're through."

He reached forward to grab at Rosie, but she stood her ground. She let go of the breath she'd been holding, and as it flowed out of her in a strangled cry of "You asshole!" something else flowed out of her as well.

A long bolt of that same crackling electricity that she'd seen coming out of Declan sparked from her fingertips. She stretched out her arms in front of herself to reach through the wards, and when she connected— the skin of her palms pressing to the skin of Randy's neck—it was like nothing she had ever felt before. A rush of energy broke the banks of her doubt, flowing like a torrent through her and into him. It was like an orgasm but a million times more sensitive and edging on painful. It jolted her as though trying to pull every bit of itself from her body.

Randy flew backward away from her, and he must have squeezed his gun, because it went off, a bullet disappearing into the woods around them as he hit the ground. The bikers on the lawn let go of Declan, who rushed to her side to face off against them together. The other bikers now had their handguns drawn, and while some of them pointed them their way, the others helped Randy to his feet.

Rosie knew Maggie would have heard the shot. *Please, please let her stay inside*, she begged.

"Well, what the actual fuck," Randy said, out of breath, as he came back to the front of the group. He breathed heavily but didn't seem eager to let his men know what his eyes said: he was frightened.

"Seems to me we got ourselves a live one now, don't we?" He said more to his men than to her. "Didn't know you had it in ya to push me like that, darlin'."

He looked at Declan but nodded at Rosie. "She's a firecracker alright—long as you don't let her feel all washed up and useless. Cos then she's drier than a week-old hotdog bun."

"You fuckin'—" Declan growled, moving to slip past Rosie so that he could attack Randy.

"Whoa there," Randy laughed as the bikers leveled their weapons straight at Declan's chest. "Who the hell are you, friend?"

"I'm Rosie's King," Declan said coolly, staring him down. "Who the fuck are you?"

Randy whistled. "Her King?" He tilted his head to look at Rosie. "That's some messed-up Paddy-kink you got goin' on there, honey."

"Don't 'honey' me," she spat. "You lost that right a long goddamned time ago, Randy."

Randy laughed, and the sound grated on Rosie just like it had every time Randy had done something unkind or cruel in the years they had spent together.

Randy lifted his chin. "Take it away, boys."

Randy's bikers fired their guns.

Rosie heard the click of the bullets in the chambers and felt the vibration of the sound as they left the barrels as though she was in some strange, underwater state. She braced herself for the inevitability of impact, but it didn't come. Instead, she felt the gentle embrace of energy surrounding her – her wards and Declan's protection – and then she heard the clatter of the bullets against magic.

But the magic couldn't hold.

As the bikers kept firing, the shield of energy began to falter. Rosie felt the strength of her wards starting to fail and looked to Declan with panic in her eyes. She reached for his hand, intending to run for the relative safety of the cottage, but she was too late. A single bullet managed to pierce the protective blanket of magic around them. He stumbled backward, looking down at his shirt as a bright red stain began to spread outwards from the bullet wound.

"No!" Rosie cried, lunging for Declan as he fell to the ground. She pressed a hand to the wound in his chest, and he met her gaze as the bullets continued to pepper the quickly fading wards.

"Get—Maggie," he grunted at her, worming his fingers beneath hers so that she could go. And then he turned his attention back to the bikers. Rosie could feel him starting to gather energy from all around them, and she knew in that instant that he meant to stay so that she and Maggie could get away.

This was it. She knew that now. This was the penultimate moment when she had to decide whether to keep running or accept her fate.

"Mom!"

Maggie's panicked cry from way behind her on the porch helped her make her decision in a heartbeat. Rosie turned back to the bikers and began pulling in energy much as Declan was, but she wasn't wounded. She threw the full force of her magic forward in one sudden blast. It passed through the wards and knocked Randy and his men to the ground in one fell swoop.

"What the fuck?" Randy yelled, scrambling back to his feet. He was breathing hard again, staring, white-faced. He gestured at her with the gun, but she didn't feel afraid at all.

"My guys," he stuttered, taking stumbling steps backward. "They had some wild story about what happened at your place that day they came up here, but I didn't—"

"What? Think it was true?" Rosie finished his thought for him. "Well, it *was* true, Randy. All of it."

She fixed a slow, menacing smile onto her face and began to stalk toward him. She didn't know what

Randy's men had experienced when they had come to vandalize the cottage or burn down Declan's camper, but she would claim it all. It had all been her in origin, after all.

"I ran off those sonsabitches and let them live so that they could warn you away from coming up here yourself. But, of course," she barked a laugh, "you're too damn slow to take the hint." She held up her hands as though it would illustrate her point.

"I'm a witch."

Randy had been taking two steps back for each Rosie had taken forward, his gun dangling from his hand as he tried to maintain some distance between them. But when she finished, he stopped. He started a spluttering laugh that the other bikers joined in on, horrible high-pitched laughs like hyenas in a kids' movie.

Rosie felt hot all over, and like she'd eaten an entire turkey with all the trimmings. She was so full, and so warm, that for a moment she swayed on her feet. She felt power surge from her bare feet in the grass and from the sun beaming brightly up above.

In one massive intake, Rosie summoned all her arcane energy and then threw her hands forward straight in the direction of Randy to release it.

Every insult he had hurled, every bruise he had caused, every flash of anger she had felt over the last two decades came out in the energy she shot at him. It was as though she worked backward in time: His shooting on her new cottage, with Maggie inside. His threatening her. His burning down Declan's camper, to scare her if not to harm Declan. Pulling her by the hair and throwing her into bed. Keeping their money in his own account, so she couldn't have access to it. Telling her that they weren't the type of people to raise kids and that she should 'get rid of it.'

The bikers convulsed on the ground as she poured every heartache out, until other things started to come out of her. Late-night conversations about dreams which would never come true. The way he used to smile at her when they were kids, before drugs and bad choices had turned him from a bad boy into just plain bad. The moment Maggie was born, and the look of pride on his face when he held his child for the first time.

She felt a small hand on her forearm.

"Mom..." Maggie was by her side. Her daughter's softness and gentle spirit felt so different from the white-hot hatred Rosie felt for Randy, and she realized it was Maggie's presence in her energy field that had brought the less painful memories to the front of her mind. Rosie kept her magic focused on Randy, but listened to the small, sweet voice beside her.

"If we do bad things like they do," she said, "then we'll deserve all the bad things that have happened to us."

Rosie felt Maggie's grip around her arm tighten. She kept her other arm outstretched, fingers pointing at Randy. But Maggie's face tore at her conscience.

Grey eyes like Rosie's but flecked with brown like Randy's gazed up her, brimming with tears. "You said it, remember?" Maggie tugged on her arm, trying to break her concentration. "No more bad things from now on!"

Her magic was almost spent. She felt it ebbing away, but it was still strong enough to finish the job she had started. At the very last moment, when Randy was just about to slip into pale, redeeming death, Rosie relented. She fell to her knees beside Declan on the ground. With one hand on the lawn in front of her for balance, Rosie slipped her free arm around Maggie and drew her daughter close.

"You have your daughter to thank for keepin' your life," she told Randy, glaring at him where he lay curled up like a worm in the dirt. "Now, you're finally gonna do right by her."

Instead of focusing on the world around Randy and removing him from it, Rosie focused on adding to Randy instead. She pushed her thoughts out, surrounding Randy until he was covered in a speeding whir of bright green light. As the energy grew smaller and the magic diminished, there was nothing left of Randy except a pile of dirty clothes, moving on the lawn.

Maggie gasped beside her. "Declan!"

Rosie spun to look and regretted it instantly because her vision continued to spin long after she had stopped. When she managed to focus, she saw that Declan's eyes were half-closed, and his face was beetroot red.

What if he was dead? *Oh God, please don't let him be dead.*

Shuffling closer on her knees until she was beside him with Maggie hovering nervously next to her, Rosie placed her hands on Declan's chest. She could still feel a heartbeat, but it was faint and getting fainter by the second.

"Mom, you're a witch. Can't you help him?"

Rosie closed her eyes and summoned whatever energy she had left. She thought about the butterflies she had felt in her stomach when he had texted her, asking if she needed a ride home from work. She thought of the way he had enlisted Maggie's help to repair the porch deck. And then she thought about how they had kissed each other in the meadow, surrounded by fireflies and moonlight.

Repairin' things is all about findin' a little love for it.

Her energy poured from her splayed hands straight into him, spreading through his veins, healing as it went. She felt his heartbeat getting stronger, slowly at first, and then with an intensity that increased as her magic dwindled. Rosie took a deep breath and then pushed the remainder of her gratitude toward him through the connection. She fell back against the ground as Maggie looked into Declan's face.

"You did it!" she declared.

The three of them sat in silence for what felt like forever. Rosie could feel tears of exhaustion and emotion streaming down her face, but underneath them was a smile. Proud and relieved, she pushed the tears away. *She did it*. She took Maggie's hand.

Declan sat up, holding onto his side as though it pained him.

"I'm so proud of you," he murmured. He reached to cover their hands with one of his.

ROSIE WAS VAGUELY AWARE OF RANDY'S CRONIES picking each other up, their motorcycles rumbling as they took off down the road. Maggie helped her to her feet, and then together, they worked to do the same for Declan. She was glad he could stand because she was fading fast. She stumbled, and his arm tightened around her waist.

"Whoa," he murmured, adjusting his grip. "You alright there?"

"I'm just glad we're all okay," she smiled up at him, her eyes finding it hard to focus. She felt so tired, so spent that even the effort of blinking was almost too much for her.

"But what about Dad?" Maggie asked, pausing to look back.

"He'll keep," Rosie said, her voice dipping into a flat tone before she corrected herself and met Maggie's confused look. "Why don't you go see for yourself, Pumpkin."

"What have you done?" Declan grinned, brushing her bangs to the side of her face as Maggie dashed back toward the pile of clothes.

"No less than he deserved," Rosie muttered, then smirked. "Figured it was time for him to stick his neck out for his kid."

"Mom!" Maggie's excited voice cut across to them, and she came running up the lawn holding a small round thing in her grip. "He's a turtle?! Can I keep him?"

Declan began to chuckle as Rosie's smirk broke into a grin. "Only if you want to, Pumpkin."

"Awesome!" Maggie danced ahead with her new 'pet', forgetting the adults behind her in her youthful enthusiasm.

"That's one way to keep him from being so dangerous," Declan said, bending by her side. "Come, Your Majesty."

His hands were suddenly underneath her, wiggling for a good hold. And then he scooped her up, holding her to his chest the way he had done the first night they'd met. Rosie could hear his heart thundering in his chest and the soft scent of his sweat. Something that smelled like woodsmoke and fresh rain enveloped her senses. Those were two of her favorite scents.

"What are you doing?" she asked, worried that he was going to hurt himself but too tired to object. "I only just fixed you."

"I'm fine," he replied, stifling a grunt.

She smiled weakly and let him carry her to the

house. He walked in silence, the sun rising behind the trees and casting her garden in that magical half-toned light that bathes everything pale gold before the fullness of day.

When they reached the porch, he carried her up the steps to set her down at the front door. But once she was standing, he didn't move his hands from her waist.

"You saved me," he told her, looking down into her face with an intensity that was hard to read. Was he annoyed that he'd needed saving? Upset that she'd ignored his instructions to get Maggie? Scared that her power had almost fried a guy to death? Or was it D – all of the above?

"I suppose I did," she said.

He gazed at her in wonder. "Rosie, I've never seen any witch show as much power as *you* just did. You are a powerful fuckin' witch." His voice was soft and lilting, barely a whisper. "And more than that – you're the witch that all the witches in the world will look up to. Whether ya know it right now, or not."

"Even you?"

"Especially me."

Declan lifted his hand to her cheek, letting it hover there for a moment as he drank in the sight of her. And then he bent down, stooping to place a soft, fleeting kiss on her lips that Rosie was just thinking about deepening as they were bumped from the side.

Maggie dashed past them. "Sorry!" she called back, charging into the house, turtle in hand.

CHAPTER FIFTEEN

Rosie carried a bowl of potato salad wrapped in her arms as she made for the front door. She passed the living room, humming to herself.

"Hrrksss!"

"Arrgh!"

She nearly tripped over the turtle that had once been her ex. She corrected herself and saved the potato salad, glaring as she stepped away from him.

"Did you seriously just *hiss* at me?" she asked in a crisp, no-nonsense tone.

He stared her down. His beady, emotionless eyes were barely any different to when he had been a human. A few weeks as a reptile clearly hadn't changed him much for the better.

Rosie raised an eyebrow. "It's not too late for me to

turn you into a toad and leave you out in a field for a hawk, y'know," she told him pointedly.

They had tied a cat toy to his shell so that he couldn't escape under any furniture, but he still wasn't allowed out of his tank without supervision.

"Maggie!" Rosie yelled as she stepped through the screen door. "You know you're not allowed to let the turtle roam the house!"

"Sorry, Mom!" Maggie yelled right back, abandoning the tire swing Declan had hitched up for her in the old oak tree. She ran for the cottage, aiming to sprint past Rosie as she came down the porch steps.

"Don't run up the steps," she told her daughter, who reluctantly slowed down. Rosie fixed her with a look before she could escape. "You're gonna have to come up with a name for that thing, you know."

Maggie pouted. "Why can't I just call him Dad?" she asked.

"Because it's weird." Rosie pulled a face, wrinkling her nose. "Now hush, before someone overhears you. Go put him away."

"Yes, ma'am," Maggie said, making for the door.

"And don't let the—" Rosie said, interrupted by the screen door banging shut behind her child. "—screen slam."

The showdown with Randy seemed so far away. Life had settled down some since then. Unfortunately, the heat still pervaded no matter how much Rosie was looking forward to a change in the weather.

Maggie was blooming. She had embraced living in the cottage with gusto, running through the very edges of the woods and enjoying the start of school. Declan had been marvelous with Maggie, helping her craft a turtle enclosure for her room and find rocks and other odds and ends to fill it with.

They'd decided to have a good old-fashioned cook-out that afternoon, to celebrate the fresh coat of paint going on the cottage. Matthew Bishop and his buddies were working with paintbrushes in hand and had almost finished the first coat of a pretty yellow that Rosie knew was going to look incredible with fresh white trim once they were done.

Rosie thought manual labor was a much better solution than having to involve the police in the egging incident. Prissy had eventually agreed, though Rosie suspected the Pastor had a hand in it. There was a certain amount of poetic justice to it all – if Rosie squinted hard enough, the yellow reminded her of a pastel version of egg yolk. And as Prissy herself had pointed out the first time she had visited Fox Cottage, busy was the only way to be.

Rosie had just stepped onto the lawn when Declan's voice drifted to her from the grill.

"Uh... Rosie?"

She looked up at the tone of his voice. Tammy Holt was standing not far away from him, her face puffy and red from crying. Rosie looked at the woman in confusion, and then her eyes fell to Tammy's hand, clutched in front of the laundry bag full of clothes she hugged in front of her.

Tammy wasn't wearing her wedding ring.

Thanks for reading

Thanks so much for reading New Witch on the Block. I hope you enjoyed the beginning of Rosie's story as much as I enjoyed writing it!

When my brain first presented me with the question 'what if a single mum discovered that she was actually a witch?', I had no idea that it would snowball the way it did. It wasn't long before the idea was cemented in my imagination, involved magical royalty, a fresh start from a bad past, and a wannabe lover that would make us want to swoon and want to slap him in equal measure.

Rosie is one of those characters who took hold of my imagination and just wouldn't let go. Her whole entourage arrived in a similar fashion, and I am so grateful to be able to share headspace with her—and I can't wait to see what she gets up to next!

The next book in the series, *Jealousy's A Witch*, delves deeper into her growing relationship with Declan and her life as a mother, as well as exploring Rosie's foray into her own powers. Read on to enjoy the first chapter!

I'd love to have you along for the ride.

Louisa xo

Bless your heart

It takes a village to raise a child. Apparently it takes one to write a book, too!

Thank you to my editor and fellow author Kimberly Jaye, for helping me make sense of the story I wanted to tell, and busting her hump to make it happen.

Thanks also to my other author pal, Lana Pecherczyk, for pushing me to put the book up for preorder and then alternately freaking out and doing writing sprints with me until it was done.

I'm lucky to have a wonderful network—thank you to Courtney Owston, Natasha Devereux, Sonia Bellhouse, Elizabeth Ellen Carter, Megan Mayfair, Rachael Johns, Sarah Sloan, Laura Timmer, and Tiff Hastie for their fabulous contributions to my worldbuilding.

My wonderful partner's input and advice to 'just keep chipping away at it' were both delightful and frustrating in equal measure—thanks for your support, Lindsay.

Lastly, thank you to my beautiful daughter Elizabeth, who helped make my Mosswood map and who loves the characters in the book almost as much as I do.

Love it? Review it!

A reader writing a review for a book is such a gift to an author. Not only does it let us know that someone out there actually read the thing, but it's so heart-warming to think that they enjoyed it enough to offer their thoughts on it afterwards.

If you've enjoyed this book, I would be so grateful if you'd consider leaving me a review! You can do this by searching for the book title and my name on Amazon.com or on GoodReads and then following the prompts.

If you're a book-blogger, bookstagrammer, or journalist and you would like to interview me, please get in touch with me at www.louisawest.com - I would love to chat with you!

Your next Mosswood adventure awaits!

JEALOUSY'S A
WITCH

MIDLIFE IN MOSSWOOD BOOK 2

Available now on Amazon and in Kindle Unlimited

https://books2read.com/jaw

Jealousy's A Witch

She thought the thriller part of her life was behind her. But when the man she's falling for has a sinister secret, she's no longer sure whether he's a trick or a treat.

Rosemary Bell is a witch for Halloween... and every other day of the year. And that's not even the weirdest thing about her life. Her ex-husband is a turtle, her daughter Maggie's new best friend is an imaginary kangaroo, and the guy sleeping on her couch is a King —as well as her fated lover.

Just as she's starting to fall for Declan, Rosie gets spooked by a revelation that leaves her wondering whether she is really meant to be his Queen. And as a new houseguest quickly proves, promises don't always mean forever. When a sexy blast from the past arrives in town with her eyes set on Rosie's King and crown, she will have to decide for herself what her destiny is, and soon.

Struggling between caring for Declan and caring for herself, Rosie has better luck advising her friends what to do about their love lives than tending to her own. But when Maggie goes missing on All Hallow's Eve, Rosie is forced to admit that jealousy's a witch - literally!

***The Good Witch* meets *Hocus Pocus* in this short**

novel about stepping into new shoes, choosing who you're going to be, and never letting fear decide your fate, even on Halloween.

AVAILABLE NOW

https://books2read.com/jaw

Jealousy's A Witch - Chapter One

I t felt as though the whole world was holding its breath. Aside from the sound of Maggie singing to herself inside the cottage and the hiss and spit of the meat on the grill, everything was silent. Even the boys painting the house had stopped their chatter, turning to peer at the new arrival with unrestrained interest. Rosie looked from Tammy to Declan and then back again, trying to simultaneously assess the situation and form a plan before everything went to hell in a handbasket.

But life was never meant to be that easy—or at least hers wasn't. Rosie tried to take a deep breath, but the air around her was robbed of oxygen. Instead the atmosphere was charged with all the tension of a gathering storm, as though everything in her life had been leading her right up to that very moment. All of the disappointments and heartbreaks she had suffered seemed like training hurdles, and as her eyes met Tammy's she knew that this situation was somehow the test she hadn't realized she'd been waiting for all along. Her own energy seemed to twist and turn inside of her, rushing to the edge of release before shying back away from the final leap.

She thought back to the day she had met Tammy, huddled amongst the stronger personalities of Priscilla Bishop, the Pastor's wife, and Leanne Coombes as they had invaded her home under the guise of welcoming her to Mosswood. She had seemed like the only genuine person in the bunch. Rosie had felt terrible when Tammy had seen her husband Terry making a pass at her the day he'd come out to the cottage to 'offer his services' as a handyman. She hadn't seen her since that day, but it didn't look like things had improved for her any.

Tammy looked sheepishly between Declan and Rosie, her knuckles tight around the laundry bag of clothes she held in front of her like a trick or treat sack.

"I don't mean to impose," she said softly, even though it was clear that she knew she was. "I hoped that...well!" Unshed tears suddenly welled in her eyes, and she tried a combination of blinking and fanning her wedding-ring devoid hand in front of her face to stop them from falling.

Declan shifted uncomfortably beside the grill. He turned his attention to the meat intently, but Rosie could see the tense setting of his shoulders. Tammy was glancing between the pair of them, clearly embarrassed and unsure of what to say or do.

Rosie's heart squeezed for Tammy. She wasn't one to leave someone in distress without a shoulder to cry on, and as she took her first step across the lawn it felt as though something deep inside of her resonated with her decision to help Tammy. She crossed to the table and set down the potato salad.

"Declan, could you please get another table setting and some wine from inside?"

He abandoned the grill with relief, offering Rosie a grateful but subdued smile as he headed for the house. She wasn't sure what this conversation was about to entail, but at least now Declan and Maggie wouldn't interrupt before Tammy had the chance to pour out the details.

"Why don't you have a seat?" Rosie gestured to the table, "and I'll pour us some lemonade," she suggested.

A light breeze picked up in the very tops of the trees, sending the woods into a gentle cascade of whispers that chased away the stillness in the air. One of the boys let out a snort of laughter at something one of his buddies had said, and a bird called across the lawn to its mate. Rosie glanced up as she poured the drinks, feeling the pressure of her own energy melting away. She looked over at Tammy, searching for a sign that the other woman had picked up on the subtle magic that had just happened right in front of her.

She didn't seem to have noticed and had settled

herself at the table, swiping at the tears now streaking down her face. The glass of lemonade being sat before her seemed to give her the confidence she needed to carry through with the story.

"I'm so sorry to barge in on y'all like this," she sniffled, "but I didn't know where else to go. You were so kind the day we all came out here. And I could use a little of your courage."

Her gaze jumped to the teenagers currently slinging pale yellow paint at each other as they painted Rosie's cabin, a punishment imposed after they had egged her and her daughter when they first came to Mosswood. Rosie glanced over at them, too, and had a feeling it was one of the teens' mothers, Priscilla Bishop, Tammy was really thinking of.

"You don't need to apologize," Rosie told her, taking a seat beside her at the picnic table Declan had built. "So let's get that out of the way right now. We're just having a cook-out, and you're officially invited."

Rosie's acceptance of Tammy sparked a chain reaction inside of her. It started as a small, warm tingle in her heart that radiated outwards, gathering more heat as it went. In no time at all it felt like it covered her entire body. Try though she might to hold it in, Rosie could feel her control starting to slip. The sensation of magic beginning to leak from her body was enough to incite a spike of panic; she couldn't risk showing her powers in front of Tammy and a bunch of local teenagers.

But the spike was enough of a hiccup to open up a

bigger release. Energy spouted out of Rosie and up into the sky, making the leaves of the trees shudder as it dissipated into the atmosphere. But what goes up, as the saying went, must come down. The magic drifted back to the earth like snowflakes; shimmering energy that was only just barely visible to Rosie as she squinted at it. It settled like a comforter across the lawn, sending out an aura of approval that Rosie felt through to her very core. She thought back to what Declan had said, that night on the porch when he had informed her that she was the Queen of the Lost.

Was this what it felt like, to be taking steps forward into accepting that mantle?

Tammy finished wiping her eyes and offered a weak smile in return. "Thank you."

Rosie smiled back. "You're welcome. Now," she added, leaning towards Tammy with a soft expression. "Why don't you tell me all about it?"

Tammy nodded slowly and looked down at her hands clasped in her lap.

"Well. I went to the Church to drop off a batch of cookies I'd made for Sunday School," she began. "I came into the kitchen through the side door, so I guess he didn't hear me. The pantry door was open, and when I poked my head around in to see if anyone was inside, there he was with his pants around his ankles." She rolled her eyes toward Rosie. "I'd know his pasty butt anywhere."

Tammy looked up and down the ridge toward Mosswood. "In a town this small, you hear things."

Rosie smiled wryly. "Ain't that the truth."

Tammy laughed through the remnants of her tears, but then shook her head. "I've been hearin' for years about Terry runnin' around behind my back. But anytime I confronted him, he denied it. And I believed him. But seeing him with someone else, I knew all the rumors were true, and had been all this time."

Her tears ran anew, and Rosie pulled the apron from around her waist and handed it to her to use as a hand-kerchief. Tammy took it gratefully and wiped her eyes as she continued. "He followed me home, but I couldn't listen to him." She glanced at the laundry bag next to her on the table. "I just grabbed whatever I could reach and jumped in the car. Almost slammed his hand in the door."

Rosie interjected. "No more than he deserved."

She looked up at Rosie as though remembering herself and shook her head. "I can't believe how nice you're being. That day I saw you and Terry—"

Rosie interrupted. "That was all on Terry."

"—which I know now!" Tammy said. "I knew it the minute we got home. He made all the same excuses then as he did today, so I knew he'd been lying then, too." She looked up at Rosie. "I'm sorry."

"Don't be," Rosie breathed. "None of this is your fault."

"I know," Tammy agreed more forcefully than Rosie would have suspected the softly spoken woman capable of. "I don't know whether I'm more sad or angry or just happy to be rid of him, but I do know that."

Rosie nodded knowingly. She remembered how she had felt when she'd reached the last straw with Randy and finally decided she was leaving him. It was like the last rubber band he had placed around her heart had snapped, letting the circulation back in. She reached out to place her hand on top of Tammy's and inspected her face.

"Can I offer you a little advice from someone who recently left her husband?"

"Please!" Tammy cried, dabbing at her eyes. "I don't know what to do with myself now."

"I know it's hard to let go of everything you'd hoped the relationship would be," she said, squeezing Tammy's hand. "But looking back is no way to move forward. From now on, things aren't *about* Terry anymore. They're about you."

Tammy looked up into Rosie's face. "I married Terry straight out of high school. I don't even know who I am except his wife."

Rosie dipped her head to one side, fixing Tammy with an appraising look before she slapped a hand on the table. "No time like the present to find out."

She stood, hoping her momentum of activity would transfer into Tammy and distract her from the shock she'd had. She planted her hands energetically on her hips, like Wonder Woman. "Now. Why don't you put your things inside and help me finish the side salad?"

Tammy looked at the cabin and then back at Rosie. "Oh, no. I couldn't! You've got enough on your plate without takin' me in."

Rosie leaned forward to take Tammy's hand in both of hers, looking into the other woman's doe-like eyes. "You can and you will. Now's no time to be alone, Tammy." She patted Tammy's hand. "You should be with friends."

Tammy's eyes welled up with tears again, and she squeezed Rosie's hands. But the transferring of energy seemed to work, because she stood up from the picnic table and grabbed her bag of laundry in front of her. She took a deep breath.

"Okay," she said, more determinedly than seemed appropriate for the next line out of her mouth, "Take me to the lettuce."

Rosie smiled encouragingly.

The breeze kicked up a notch as she followed Tammy to the front porch. The lawn, which was almost due for mowing, rippled under the movement. As she followed Tammy up the porch steps, Rosie felt a pair of eyes on her. She turned to look at young Matthew Bishop, who was staring so hard at the pair of them that she thought he might have been trying to turn them to stone. Rosie felt a fierce protectiveness of Tammy well up inside of her. She lifted her chin by way of a silent challenge, and Matthew leaned down to dip his paint brush into his bucket again.

Her plan worked, and Tammy busied herself in the kitchen. Maggie resurfaced just in time to be given the job of setting the table, and Rosie stepped over to check that Declan wasn't burning the steaks.

"Everything okay?" he asked in a low voice, glancing up at her with a put-on smile that was entirely for Maggie's benefit.

Rosie peered at the meat. "It will be. Just needs a little time. I think you're done."

Declan pressed the steaks one more time with the barbecue tongs and then nodded. "Yep. Perfectly cooked."

"Only if you like eating charcoal," Rosie teased him. She skipped two steps ahead of him as he tried to pinch her with the tongs. A little thrill fluttered inside her as she thought about the plans she'd had for the evening, though their new house guest might have put a damper on things. She turned to look at Declan.

He looked sexy as all get-out. Grilling was such a simple task, but one that made him seem capable, determined, and a good provider all at once. The look of concentration on his rugged features was enough to give Rosie a glimpse of what he might look like focusing on other things, and she almost blushed before swatting the thought away.

They had only known each other a few weeks,

but she felt an undeniable connection with him. Finding love had been the last thing on her mind when she'd decided to leave Randy. She had Maggie to think about, and her need to get them settled into a healthy and happy lifestyle trumped everything else. But Declan had shown that he wanted those things, too.

And it didn't hurt that Declan's arm muscles bunched and stretched as he turned the meat, or that the next best thing to him facing her was her getting to look at his taut, cargo-short-clad backside uninterrupted.

Well. Almost uninterrupted.

"Gross," Maggie complained from the table, and Rosie laughed lightly. Maggie glanced at Declan, who was transferring the meat from the grill to a plate. "You're *flirting* with him."

Rosie made brief eye contact with Declan and took a deep breath. Since she started school in Mosswood, Maggie's feelings toward Declan seemed to shift and change with the weather. Rosie didn't know whether it was because kids at school talked, or that Maggie had good days with her father as a turtle, or something she or Declan did. She read the sole library book in all of Mosswood's tiny building on parenting through divorce, and it had no better advice than what she already planned to do: be gentle and kind as she sorted through her feelings, and talk if she wanted to talk.

Declan picked up the cue.

"Which steak is yours, Miss Magnolia?" he asked

ceremoniously, lowering the plate for her to pick out her meat.

Afternoon stretched into a pale, star-speckled evening. The food was good, in that filling, home-style way. Everyone at the table ate more than they should but not as much as they'd have liked, and after the dishes had been cleared the three adults sat there with their drinks while Maggie chased after fireflies with an empty Mason jar.

"This is the life I want for myself," Tammy said wistfully. "Slow and quiet."

Declan and Rosie exchanged knowing smiles across the table.

The old lanterns Rosie had found in the garden shed had been filled with cheap white candles that lit the table just enough for Rosie to see the yearning on Tammy's face. The half-painted cottage just visible in the fading light behind them made a mockery of the deal Rosie had made with Prissy, and the Spanish moss in the Oak tree by the table reminded her of the night Declan's camper had gone up in a blaze.

Slow and quiet? *Yeah, right.*

"It might not be easy to start with," Rosie said, watching Maggie giggle and dance across the lawn with her jar, "but you'll get there. We can start by making you a bed on the floor in Maggie's room—"

"Couch's taken," Declan added with a smirk that was part amusement, part disappointment that made Tammy smile. His eyes found Rosie's and she noticed an unasked question lingering in his gaze. He'd been staying with them in the cottage for weeks now, and undoubtedly would have liked to have moved into the bedroom. She hadn't invited him yet, but her thoughts had certainly been leaning that way over the past few days. Rosie smiled at him coyly, before forcing herself to look away.

"—and then," Rosie continued, "We'll help you get back on your feet again. Whatever you might decide that means for you."

"Well, for one thing, I'll never get up early to pack a cooler for a hunting trip again!" She said, as though only just thinking of it. "His hunting stories were—" she hesitated, looking for the right word and then, finding it, she blurted it out. "—boring!" Tammy barked a disbelieving laugh and clapped her hands over her mouth, as though she couldn't believe she'd said something unkind about her husband. And then, now that the floodgate had been opened, it seemed unlikely it would ever close again.

"Boring, boring, boring. The football he likes to watch is boring. His taste in food is boring. I've been half bored to death these last fifteen years and I didn't even know it!"

"But not anymore!" Rosie said proudly. "You can choose things for yourself, now! What do you like to watch on TV? What do you like to eat? Those are the only decisions ahead of you now!"

Tammy shook her head slightly, awe filling her large blue eyes as she met Rosie's gaze. "Thank you, Rosie." She reached across the table to take Rosie's hand. "You've proven to me that there are still good people in this world willin' to help a fellow Christian in need."

Declan swallowed a mouthful of his lemonade too quickly, and started to cough, earning him a glare from Rosie.

"Don't you worry about a thing," she told Tammy, turning to face her and ignoring Declan's obvious amusement. "You'll be just fine, you wait and see."

The breeze from earlier continued to wash around them; a soothing wave of warm fragrant air that made Rosie think of sweet grass, bare feet, and laughter. Something she couldn't explain felt like it had fallen into place. As Rosie continued to watch Maggie, her eyes darting every so often to Declan and then across to Tammy, she realized that they were all right where they were meant to be.

The dreaminess of Rosie's thoughts was interrupted by the unmistakable sound of a car burning up the road towards the cottage. Rosie frowned and looked over at Declan before training her eyes on the flash of a vehicle on the road behind the trees. Before too long, a snowy white SUV pulled off the road and into full view on the lawn. Rosie let out a steady breath to keep her cool, but it wasn't going to work.

"Here's a little of that 'slow'n easy' you were wishin' for, Tammy," Declan murmured sarcastically, pushing himself up out of his chair.

Tammy leapt up as well. "I'll just clear some of these dishes," she said, rushing to gather anything on the table that was within arm's reach.

Rosie placed a calming hand on Tammy's. "You haven't done anything wrong," she reminded her. Tammy froze, clearly trying to decide whether to give in to fight or flight. She eventually gave Rosie one anxious nod.

Rosie narrowed her eyes as she watched Prissy hop out of the car, slamming the door behind her. "Can we help you?" Rosie asked bluntly, crossing her arms over her chest.

"I came to speak to Tammy," Prissy said tartly, tossing her blonde mane over her shoulder and putting a hand on her hip. "I heard she was here, instead of home where she oughta be."

"I didn't realize you were Tammy's keeper," Rosie interjected, earning her Prissy's attention. The blonde woman's eyes narrowed down to mean little slits, and her unspoken retort was that she was *everyone's* keeper.

"Maybe you'd do well to mind your own business, Rosie," she said, feigning sweetness. "I know you're still new in town but buttin' in on people's private troubles ain't really the way things work around here."

Rosie snorted, amused. "And yet here you are," she laughed in disbelief.

"It's okay, Rosie." She turned to see Tammy standing uncertainly on the porch.

Prissy looked smugly over at Rosie as though she'd won a major victory. "A little privacy, please?" she said more than asked.

"She can stay," Tammy interjected. She looked up and met Rosie's gaze. "I want her to stay."

Prissy frowned so hard that Rosie thought she was looking for a way to earn her Botox top-up. She turned away from Rosie to cut her out of the conversation and focused on Tammy instead.

"I'm surprised you didn't come to me and Myles the *minute* you felt you were in crisis," she scolded.

"I just needed to get away from there," Tammy said, rushing on when she heard a disapproving cluck from Prissy, "—and I knew that you would just try and talk me into staying."

"Honey, you know this ain't nothin' but a blip!" Prissy moved around to sit on the porch steps beside Tammy so that she wouldn't be able to look to Rosie for support. "Remember how it was when Terry asked you to Prom? And we all thought that God's plan for you was takin' shape at last, on account of how handsome he was, and how sweet, and how driven to have his own shop?"

"I remember," Tammy said, and Rosie could tell by her voice that she was fighting back tears again.

"Well, you can't be spittin' on God's plan!" Fire sparked in Prissy's voice, and she seemed to warm to her subject. "You *have* to forgive him. Married's married - for better or worse!"

Rosie felt her body cool and prickle all over with goosebumps. She remembered the minister saying those fateful words on *her* wedding day, and if they hadn't played over and over in her mind for years then she might have been strong enough to seek her and Maggie's emancipation from Randy sooner. She bristled and turned around in a rush. Tammy and Prissy both turned to look up at her; Tammy in admiration and Prissy in shock.

"You listen to me, Prissy Bishop," Rosie said in a low voice. "When someone stays in a marriage for 'better or worse', it's usually for the worse! Tammy has every right to feel how she's feeling! She caught her husband with another woman, after years of suspecting it!" With a fierce glare, Rosie walked up on the porch and wrapped an arm around Tammy's shoulder. "Instead of comin' out here to preach to her about forgiveness, why don't you go and preach to Terry about fidelity!"

Prissy gasped loudly again, drawing the attention of Declan and the teenagers who had been cleaning up their painting tools. She stood, clutching her car keys in her manicured claws. "I'm leavin'," she said darkly, "and I'm takin' the boys with me! I don't want them picking up any wrong ideas from being around a household like this one."

"Best news I've heard all day," Rosie told her cheerfully.

The boys didn't need to be told to down tools twice. They piled into Prissy's car like the Israelites following Moses. The car took off as soon as the last door was closed, leaving them all staring at it as it vanished back down the road. Rosie gave Tammy's shoulders a gentle squeeze just as another car pulled up.

Rosie's boss, Ben, got out of the old-but-tidy sedan and gave them a perfunctory wave as he went around to the trunk to fetch out a box.

"Ben!" Maggie's excited voice cut through the night. Rosie winced and then heard the colliding of bodies as Maggie ran full speed into a hug. Ben grunted from the impact, and then Maggie's voice rang out again. "Cool! I wanna sleep on the floor!" A moment later Maggie came dashing up the porch steps with a small black air pump and an electrical cord. Ben followed after at a Mosswood Mosey.

"Why was Prissy Bishop drivin' down the road lookin' madder than a cut snake?" he asked, a smirk hovering at the edges of his lips.

"Beats me," Rosie said, squinting into the darkness at him as he approached. "That woman does a lot of things I can't make any sense of."

"Fair enough," Ben grinned, stopping in front of

Declan and holding out the box he was carrying.

"One inflatable camping mattress, as per your order. Hi Tammy," he added kindly.

Tammy looked from Ben to the mattress and back to Rosie, who shook her head.

"This one's all Declan," she said, giving Tammy one more light squeeze before releasing her.

"Thank you, Ben," Tammy said, "and you, Declan." Though the light was fading and it was getting harder to see, the emotion was clear in her voice.

"Thank me once we've actually managed to get it set up," Declan smiled.

"I'll give you a hand," Ben offered.

"And I'll fix us all a drink," Rosie added.

"Sure could use one," Ben admitted, at the exact same time as Tammy said "Oh, yes please!" Everyone smiled, and a gentle hum of laughter carried them up the porch steps and into the cottage. Rosie hung back, collecting the last few things off the table and rolling up the tablecloth. She followed, and even though her heart was full she wasn't sure it was going to be smooth sailing.

Maybe they were all where they were meant to be, but that didn't mean the world wasn't going to try to shift them out of place.

Available now on Amazon and in Kindle Unlimited
https://books2read.com/jaw

MIDLIFE IN
MOSSWOOD

PARANORMAL WOMEN'S FICTION SERIES

LOUISA WEST

Also by Louisa West

THE MIDLIFE IN MOSSWOOD SERIES

New Witch on the Block

https://books2read.com/nwotb

Jealousy's A Witch

https://books2read.com/jaw

We Witch You A Merry Christmas

https://books2read.com/wwyamc

Get Witch Quick

https://books2read/gwq

Son of a Witch

https://books2read/sofaw

About the author

Louisa likes Pina Coladas and gettin' caught in the rain. Determined to empty her brain of stories, she loves writing Paranormal Women's Fiction and other stories about kick-ass women doing whatever the hell they want to do.

She lives in Mandurah, Western Australia, and drinks more coffee than is good for her. When she's not writing or researching projects, Louisa enjoys spending time with her family, and Harriet The Great (Dane). Hobbies include playing video games, watching copious amounts of tv, and various craft-related initiatives.

She strongly believes that the truth is still out there.

Are you interested in:

- New release information and pre-order links
- Competitions, giveaways, and other freebies
- Sneak peeks at cover reveals and excerpts
- VIP access to online launch parties and
- Exclusive member rewards

Then join Louisa's online reader group at
www.facebook.com/groups/magicalmayhem!

facebook.com/louisawestauthor

instagram.com/louisa_west

amazon.com/author/louisawest

goodreads.com/louisawest

pinterest.com/louisawestauthor

CPSIA information can be obtained
at www.ICGtesting.com
Printed in the USA
BVHW071234260123
657206BV00006B/167